A Night in Port Arthur

Alexander Koreis

A James and Rachel Adventure

First published in 2016 by Booksplendour

ISBN 978-0-9871982-4-2

Mobile: 0422 955 200
Email: darius.k@bigpond.com

Front cover image by THPStock, design Booksplendour
Back cover image by Andrejs Zemdega, design Booksplendour

Printed in Australia

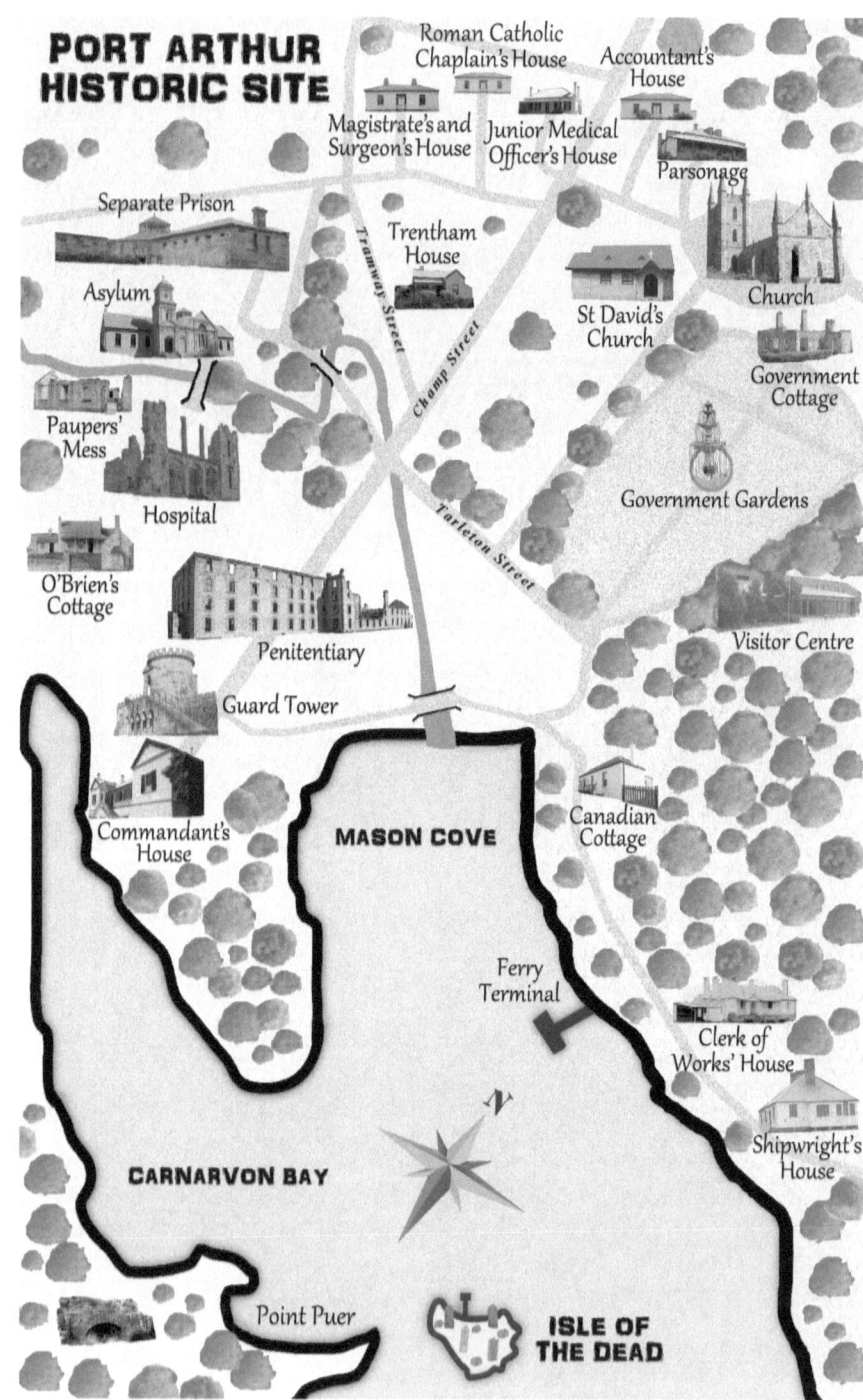

PORT ARTHUR HISTORIC SITE

Roman Catholic Chaplain's House

Accountant's House

Magistrate's and Surgeon's House

Junior Medical Officer's House

Parsonage

Separate Prison

Trentham House

Asylum

Tramway Street

Champ Street

St David's Church

Church

Government Cottage

Paupers' Mess

Tarleton Street

Hospital

Government Gardens

O'Brien's Cottage

Penitentiary

Visitor Centre

Guard Tower

Commandant's House

MASON COVE

Canadian Cottage

Ferry Terminal

Clerk of Works' House

CARNARVON BAY

Shipwright's House

N

Point Puer

ISLE OF THE DEAD

CHAPTER ONE

"This is the funniest escape ever!"

James Masters grinned mischievously, looking up from the 'Tasmanian Convict Trail' tourist brochure he'd just picked up from a rack in front of the old Officers' Quarters building at Eaglehawk Neck, Tasmania.

"Dad?" James called out behind him. "Are you listening?"

"Yes, I am." His father lifted his camera and took a photo of the old beachfront building, located about an hour's drive from Hobart.

It was a cold, windy and overcast day. An eerie mist hung in the air, hiding the tops of the mountains behind them.

"There was this guy called Billy Hunt, and he escaped from Port Arthur convict settlement," James continued. "But the problem was that Eaglehawk Neck is the only place where Port Arthur connects to the rest of Tasmania."

James' dad quickly snapped a photo of his son talking.

"Quit it, Dad," James winced when the bright flash went off unexpectedly in his face. "Anyway, Billy escaped from the prison, and the only way to get away was through here." He looked out across the building's weathered verandah and to the water either side of them. "It's only a hundred and thirty metres wide at the narrowest point with water on both sides. So the military threw everything they had at this spot to guard it."

James' mother walked up to them, cradling his two-year-old sister Emily in her arms. Her heels chattered along the wooden floor. "And not many people knew how to swim in those days," she added. "So unless they could steal a boat, they had to go by land."

"Hey, just who's telling the story here?" James playfully poked his tongue out at her. "Anyway, so the military were out here on guard twenty-four hours a day, and when Billy Hunt escaped he knew he had a problem getting past them."

"So what did he do?" his dad asked.

"He got a kangaroo skin, dressed himself up in it, and began hopping past the guards," James exclaimed. "But there was a problem."

"Oh?" his dad asked, smirking. "He tripped over his own tail?"

James laughed. "No. There was another security measure in place. They used to have a thing called the 'dog line', which was literally a line of starving dogs. The idea was that they'd alert the soldiers if they saw or smelled someone who was trying to escape."

"Oh no; I can see where this is going," his dad said. "The dogs attacked him?"

James grinned and shook his head. "No, it's better than that. The dogs started barking when they saw Billy hopping past. But the guards were hungry as well, and in their eyes they saw dinner hopping past. So they got their guns to shoot the 'kangaroo'. But Billy saw what they were going to do and stopped. He tore off his costume as quickly as he could and yelled out, 'It's only me, Billy Hunt!'"

His parents roared with laughter. "Oh, that poor man. He came so close to escaping. What happened to him?"

James' face soured as he read the rest of the story from the brochure. "He got one hundred lashes with the cat o' nine tails."

"What's that? Some kind of whip?" his mum asked.

"At school we learnt that it's a whip with knots on the end of each tail. It's an extreme form of punishment. Apparently it's still used in some countries."

"How awful, poor Billy Hunt," his mum moaned. "Change the conversation, *please*."

His dad suggested that they take a look inside the building. They began strolling through the front door, but just as his mum walked inside his baby sister began crying hysterically.

His mum tried soothing her but nothing she did worked.

However, as soon as she stepped outside Emily stopped crying. James' mum then tried taking her indoors again, but after only one step inside she started screaming again.

"It's probably best that you two go and take a look around by yourselves," his mum said sadly. "If I take her inside she'll probably shake the old place apart with all of the noise she's making."

James rolled his eyes. Apparently it was called the "terrible twos" – when kids really start to noticing the world around them. Unfortunately most of what they see is completely new to them, so it's understandable that they don't really like it and are scared of it – and that's when the tantrums start. But knowing that didn't make James' eardrums feel any better. So far little Emily had made his Tasmanian holiday a living hell. If she stayed outside at least he'd get a few minutes of peace inside.

Walking in, the first room of the house had fading wallpaper, but the walls were mostly covered with information displays, telling the story of the area and the old building.

While his dad read the wall displays, James looked at the pamphlet he'd picked up outside and continued reading. Built in 1832, just after Port Arthur prison first began, the Officers' Quarters is the oldest wooden military building left standing in Australia.

"Apparently there used to be a railway here as well," his dad told him, reading off a display board. "But they didn't use a steam engine. They used one of those old hand-pulley systems that you had to push up and down to make it move. Naturally the convicts were the ones doing all the hard work."

"Yikes," James exclaimed. "I'll take a modern electric train instead, thanks."

Stuffing the brochure into his pocket, James walked into the next room, leaving his dad to take some photos. His father, a geologist, was a keen photographer. But instead of taking photos of rocks like his job would suggest, he was obsessed with taking photos of trees. Between his screaming sister and his dad constantly stopping their campervan to take photos of trees, for two weeks he'd slowly been going out of his mind.

James came up to a wall display about the dog line. Apparently there were up to a dozen dogs covering the line. That meant one nearly every ten metres. They even put them out on platforms on the water – just to make sure that convicts didn't try escaping through the shallow breakwater either.

He closed his eyes for a moment, trying to imagine the scene. Between the dogs and the armed soldiers, it would have been quite a sight. He continued reading the information board, and it said that the dog line actually used to be a tourist attraction back in the day.

James walked into the next room, to find there was a fireplace filled with ashes and coals that looked like it had just been used yesterday. Next to it was a little staircase that led to a roof cavity, which he gingerly climbed up. The little space allowed visitors to see how the roof was constructed. Over the years it had extra support beams and struts added to it many times. A lot of the timbers looked very frail and brittle – like the balsa wood used for model airplanes.

"This place could use a dusting," James murmured.

Walking back downstairs, his dad was taking a photo of the fireplace. "Have you noticed how low the doorways are, Dad?"

"Yeah, they used to be a lot shorter in those days because they had poorer nutrition. At your age you'd already fit right in with the adults back then."

James was pretty tall for his age. At 14 years old he was in high school, and was in the middle of a growth spurt. He had brown hair and eyes, just like his dad. He may have been tall enough to fit in with the convicts, but unlike the shabby clothes they used to wear, today he wore blue jeans and a thick grey jacket. During winter, Tasmania was freezing compared to his home in Brisbane. It was especially bad with the wind along the coast – the cold blasts just never stopped. He'd never been so cold in his life.

He walked into the next room, feeling like he had to stoop under the door frame, and came across a room with a mock-up presentation of how the area looked at its busiest during the 1800s.

There had once been a long jetty, a store house, a guard house, the officers' house that he was in now, a military barracks for all of the lower-ranked soldiers, a semaphore for sending signals between Port Arthur and Hobart, a customs hut, and sentries boxes with the dog line. As many as twenty-five soldiers used to be stationed there, plus a couple of officers. In all, it had been a very busy spot, with a lot of buildings in a very small area.

Looking out of the window, he felt sorry for the soldiers who'd been stationed there. Eaglehawk Neck was barely above sea level. Waves lash the shoreline during storms, and there is no natural shelter from the howling wind. The sentries would have been exposed out in the open twenty-four hours a day while they kept an eye out for escaping convicts. James shivered at the thought. At least the soldiers were British, so they would've been used to the cold – unlike him!

The next room told the story of the end of Eaglehawk Neck as a military station. The soldiers withdrew in 1859, but local police stayed on at the site for another eighteen years until the prison at Port Arthur was closed in 1877. While most of the buildings outside fell into decay and collapsed, the Officers' Quarters went on to be a private home for a while, and that was why it managed to survive.

On the wall sat a ghostly old black and white photo of one of the families that once lived there. The way they looked at the camera was deeply haunting.

He just couldn't bear looking at it. "Creepy..."

James left the room, but saw that there was only one room left in the building. This room was dark, with no electric lights, and the window was covered over. It was completely dark apart from the slither of light coming from the small doorway, and it took a moment for his eyes to adjust.

He stepped into the room, wanting to discover what was in there. It was almost too gloomy to see, but he could make out an old couch in the corner. He sat down on it and could see all the way down the long corridor – the entire length of the house. His dad had just stepped into the previous room, and was looking at the old photos.

"Is there anything in that last room, James?" he asked.

"Nah, only a lumpy old couch. I can't see anything on the walls – it's too dark."

"Okay, in that case I better check on your mother and Emily."

He watched his dad walk back through the house, all the way to the front door. James closed his eyes for a moment, enjoying the complete peace and quiet.

Suddenly something didn't feel right. It was like ... he wasn't alone in the room anymore? A cold chill ran down his spine and he quickly opened his eyes, but he couldn't see or hear anyone in the darkness. Maybe he just imagined it?

Don't be stupid, he thought to himself. *It's probably just the wind.* He stopped breathing and concentrated on listening for a sound.

But there was nothing.

Instead a cold draft ran past his cheek and nose, and something quickly brushed past his hand – as light as a feather – but he felt his skin turn icy cold.

All of his senses went into overdrive. Some ancient instinct told him that something was very wrong.

Just then his father's head popped through the front door at the other end of the house. "James! C'mon, we're leaving," he waved at him.

James didn't hesitate for a moment. He leapt up off the couch, and with his shoes pounding against the old floorboards he bolted down the length of the house, not daring to look back.

CHAPTER TWO

James' day had soon gone from bad to worse. His parents had planned on going on a whale watching tour, but the company running the tours said his sister was too young to be allowed on the boat in rough weather. So his parents decided that none of them would go.

Instead they went to see some of the sights on land, and they visited the other tourist traps around Eaglehawk Neck: Tasman's Arch, the Tessellated Pavement and the Devil's Kitchen.

The views of the natural rock formations were admittedly spectacular – his geologist dad was in heaven – but it would have been so much cooler seeing it all from the sea. At least his father had a field day with his camera. And the trees ... so many trees. James rolled his eyes just thinking about it.

Missing out on the cruise was disappointing, but nothing compared to his sister throwing up on him as they were heading to the caravan park in Carnarvon – just down the road from Port Arthur, where they were going to spend the night. Amazingly, she didn't get a drop of it on the rented campervan's interior. James had been her sole victim.

...

James stepped out of the shower, sniffing his arm and wincing. He swore he could still smell his sister on him, but hoped that it was just his imagination. He'd spent ten minutes furiously scrubbing his arms in the caravan park's shower, and his irritated skin had turned bright red.

"What a way to end your school holidays," he grumbled to himself.

They were due to fly back to Brisbane in two days. The plan was to save the best bit of the holiday to last: Port Arthur. Tomorrow they'd spend the entire day at one of the most famous historical sites in Australia, and fly back home the day after. James would then start the new school term on Monday. Unfortunately, on today's form the end of his holiday was looking as bad as the rest had been. He almost preferred to be back at school... Almost.

But it would be such a shame to let the day's events get to him, and spoil the best part of the trip. He'd been to St Helena Island off Brisbane – another convict settlement, and absolutely loved it. Visiting these sites was as close as you can get to touching the past. He was determined for the best part of the holiday not to be ruined. "Tomorrow's another day," he tried motivating himself as a drop of water trickled down his nose.

He changed into a new set of clothes and walked out of the shower block; still drying his hair against the towel. It was getting late in the afternoon, and the temperature was dropping alarmingly.

Quickly walking to their hired campervan, James noticed that the caravan park was next to a bushland recreational area, and there was a group of four kids his age mucking around with food and drink at a picnic table. Two boys and two girls.

Still angry at his sister, he made a snap decision to stay away from her for as long as possible, and walked up to the kids to introduce himself.

"Ahh, hi there, I'm James," he said awkwardly. He nervously shuffled the damp towel between his hands.

"Hey," the tallest boy said, giving a friendly wave. "I'm Travis." He had a really laid back surfy look, with sandy hair that went over his ears and mischievous blue eyes.

Travis held out his hand for James to shake, and then quickly pulled it back as he reached out to shake it. "Ahhh, got ya!" All of the kids laughed, making James blush and regret talking to them already.

"I'm Nick," said the second boy with a reassuring grin. He was a lot shorter and plumper, with curly red hair and freckles. His hazel eyes were hidden behind a set of glasses.

"How's it going?" James asked. Nick pressed his hands together and nodded monk-like in reply.

"Hello, don't mind those two clowns – they'll never grow up," said a pretty girl with shoulder length blonde hair and sparkling green eyes. She was sitting at the other side of the table from the boys. "My name's Rachel."

"And I'm Stacy," said the final group-member; a pale, skinny girl with brown eyes, and raven black hair that ran all the way down her back.

They all looked at each other for a moment without saying anything before Travis and Nick began snickering at some unspoken joke.

"So are you guys on holidays here as well?" James asked to break the ice.

"Nah, we all live here," Travis said. "Stacy's new, though. You only came here, what, three years ago?"

Stacy nodded silently.

"Don't mind her – she's a real quiet type. The rest of us have lived here all our lives," Travis finished.

"Can I ask where you're from?" Rachel asked with a smile.

"I'm from Brisbane," James said, sitting down at the picnic table next to her after the girls scooted over to make room for him.

"Cool, I have some family living there," she replied. "How long are you staying here?"

"Umm, we're flying back in a couple of days. Port Arthur is the final stop on our road trip."

"Oh," she frowned. "That's a shame. So how long have you been down here?"

"All of the school holidays. So nearly two weeks."

"Awesome," Nick said. "Been having fun?"

James felt the wet towel in his hands, and remembered his sister's deadly accurate aim. "Umm, it's sure been interesting at times."

In the corner of his eye James saw his dad coming into view, camera in hand, and trying to capture some moody late afternoon photos of a pair of Yellow-Tailed Black Cockatoos sitting in a tree in front of the setting sun. He gave James a wave, but James ignored him, trying to pretend that he hadn't seen him.

"Sooo, were you out at Port Arthur today?" Travis asked.

"No, we only drove past it to get here just before. But we're going over there tomorrow."

"Cool," Rachel said with an even bigger smile than before. "Have you ever been to the site before?"

"Nope. I hadn't even been to Tasmania before, but I can't wait. I've been looking forward to it the entire trip," James enthused. "I've been to St Helena Island off Brisbane – it's like our version of Port Arthur – and it was awesome. I've wanted to come here since I was a little kid."

"What are you, some kind of history nerd?" Travis teased. Nick giggled.

He could feel Rachel looking at him, so he tried sounding cool in front of her. "*No.* Murderous convicts, highwaymen and bushrangers, whipping and iron bars. What's not to like?"

Travis seemed satisfied with the response, while Stacy let out a small "Eww". Nick and Rachel just nodded.

"Well, if you're into all that ... then you won't be afraid," Travis said, lowering his voice to a whisper.

James paused for a moment. "... Afraid of what?"

"Of going on a *ghost tour.*"

"Oh, good idea," Nick exclaimed, slapping the table in excitement. "That'll get his blood pumping. Port Arthur is terrifying at night."

"Hey, I'm surprised at you, dumbo," Rachel said across the table to Travis. "That's actually not a bad idea for once. So how about it, James? You've got to go on a ghost tour, especially if you haven't been out to the site yet... You won't know what to expect. It would be so much more awesome that way."

James hesitated, and the two boys saw it.

"What?" Travis asked in mock disgust. "Are you chicken?" Beside him Nick started clucking and flapping his arms. Rachel groaned, while Stacy looked on in quiet amusement.

"Hardly," James said, putting on a brave face.

"Are you sure? We've all been to Port Arthur at night," Travis said in a low voice, "and things happen out there..."

"Like what?" James asked, taking the bait. Nick got up, and while stretching his arms theatrically walked away from the table holding a cup.

"Well," Travis began, "one night the four of us went out there. We were walking along the waterfront when I heard a splash in the water, and then another even louder one. Apparently people have drowned in the bay, and their ghosts still haunt the waterfront. Now I'll admit that I was a little scared, but I still looked over the pier into the water, and then, all of a sudden..."

Splash!

Cold water ran all the way down James' shirt. Travis split his sides laughing, while behind him Nick fell to the ground in hysterics, dropping the now empty cup onto the grass. James' cheeks flushed red from a mixture of embarrassment and anger.

"Trust me, they're not worth the effort," Rachel said to him, rolling her eyes. "You're not the first person they've pulled stupid pranks on, and you won't be the last. At least you're actually holding a towel. It could have been worse."

"Not after the day I've been having," James grumpily replied. "Nice joke though," he said, attempting to see the humour in it. He tried drying himself down again, but his shirt was still soaked.

"Besides," Rachel comforted, "That story he just told? Never happened. They're too scared to go out there by themselves during the day, let alone at night."

"Oh yeah?" Travis mocked from across the table. "Unlike you, Rach? I bet you'd wet yourself."

Nick snorted. "*Wet* herself..." He held up the empty cup and they both started roaring with laughter again – dangerously close to having an accident themselves. Travis had a big smug grin on his face, and high-fived Nick as he sat back down on the table.

"So what do you say, James?" Rachel asked, ignoring the other two boys. "It's seriously a lot of fun. There are some really cool ghost stories."

James could feel them all looking at him expectantly. "I'll get back to you," he said. "Will you still be here in five or ten minutes? I need to ask my parents. I don't know if they already have plans for tonight or not."

"Sure, whatever," Travis said dismissively.

James quickly got up and walked over to their campervan, followed by the sound of clucking chicken noises.

CHAPTER THREE

When James stepped into the campervan his parents were fussing over his baby sister in the tiny kitchenette.

"She's sick, I'm sure of it. Just feel her forehead – she's running a temperature," his mother said in concern, cradling Emily in her arms.

"Umm, guys," James interrupted. "Can I ask you something?"

"What is it?" his mother snapped back in worry. "Can't you see that we're busy? Emily is very sick."

"I met some of the local kids, and they invited me to go on a ghost tour of Port Arthur tonight. Can I go? Please?"

"What ghost tour? I don't like the sound of that. Who are these kids?" his mother asked suspiciously.

"Those kids are fine," his father said. "I saw James talking to them just before when I was taking some shots."

But she didn't buy that. "How do you know they won't do something to you? Kidnap you, or steal your wallet?"

James' jaw dropped. "You can't be serious..." *She always does this*, he thought in despair.

"Well you don't know them very well, do you?" she said frowning. "You can't know what they're capable of. You only just met them."

"Yes, and in that short time they managed to devise a cunning plan to take over the world – starting with me, in the little unsuspecting town of Port Arthur," he said sarcastically.

His dad laughed out loud, but his mum shot him an angry look, causing him to stop laughing and quickly try to busy himself with making some food for Emily.

"Besides," she insisted, "your sister is sick, so your father and I need to stay here and look after her."

"Err, Mum, I was thinking about going by myself. I'll only be gone for a couple of hours. I'm not six years old anymore; I can take care of myself."

"Are you sure? You *can't* look after yourself." She pointed at him. "See, you're soaking wet. Change your shirt or you'll catch a cold."

James ignored her and turned his attention to his father. "Dad..."

"Maybe it wouldn't be such a bad thing," his father said carefully in his defence. "He's been stuck with us in the campervan for two weeks. It would be good for him to get some fresh air on his own."

His mother crossed her arms, and looked cranky. "And how are you going to get there? We don't want to drive you there if we can help it because of your sister being car sick."

"I'll take my bike, remember? We took it all this way on the plane, and I haven't even had a chance to ride it yet. Besides, it's only a couple of kilometres down the road, so it'll be fine."

"It would make up for missing the whale watching tour and Emily working her magic," his father added.

"Oh alright," she finally gave in. Behind her back his dad shot him a wink. "But only if you come back right away after it's finished."

"Cool," James grinned. "Thanks a lot."

James shot out of the campervan, and rushed over to the group.

"What took you so long?" Travis moaned. "Mummy afraid that her little baby would get lost?"

"You get lost, Travis," Stacy shot back.

"You wish," he returned with a sneer.

"–My baby sister is sick, that's what took so long," James managed to interrupt between their infighting.

"So can you come along?" Nick asked hopefully.

"Yeah," he replied.

"Awesome," Rachel beamed. "Well the tour starts at eight o' clock. You just need to go to the Visitor Centre at the bottom of the hill where you enter from the road. You can't miss it."

"Thanks," James smiled back.

"Well we were about to go to the local pool for a swim," Stacy said with a stretch of her arms. "Would you like to come with us?"

"Err, isn't it too cold to swim?" James asked in confusion. He was cold enough as it was without being in freezing water.

"Us locals are hard as nails," Nick boasted, thumping his chest. "We can handle it. They even throw in blocks of ice just to test us."

"—It's actually heated," Rachel corrected with a sigh.

"Oh, umm, well I'd love to, but I can't..." James stopped for a moment, trying to think of an excuse so he wouldn't tell her the real reason why he couldn't go with them for a swim. "I, err, didn't bring my swimmers with me."

Rachel frowned. "Oh well, that sucks. I guess in that case we'll be seeing you tonight."

James looked into her eyes and grinned. "You bet."

CHAPTER FOUR

James raced through the darkness on his mountain bike. He didn't want to be late for this. He had no trouble finding the turn-off to the Port Arthur site, and sped down the hill, doing wheelies over the speed bumps.

There were about two dozen cars in the car park, but he ignored them, carrying on to the bottom of the hill and easily spotting the brightly lit Visitor Centre. He hit the brakes hard and came to a stop, putting his bike down in the shrubs next to the modern building.

It was a cold night to say the least. Clouds hid the moon, adding to the atmosphere, and there was a constant chilling breeze. After his ride James was warm for now, but he'd brought his warmest jacket with him, knowing he'd quickly cool down while the already icy temperature would keep dropping throughout the night.

But he put those thoughts aside as nervous excitement built in his stomach. He'd always wanted to visit Port Arthur, and he was finally there!

He quickly walked through the automatic sliding doors at the front of the Visitor Centre, and towards the front desk to buy a ticket for the tour. His anticipation was growing by the second.

"Hey, James," a girl's voice called out behind him.

He spun around and Rachel ran up to him, wearing a bright pink jacket and fuzzy pink gloves.

"Hi there; don't worry; I already bought you a ticket." She reached into her jacket and pulled it out, handing it over to him gently.

"Aww, thanks a lot Rachel." He blushed, reaching into his pocket for his wallet–

"Don't be silly," she said, poking her tongue out. "You're my guest tonight."

"But–" he tried protesting.

"No arguing! C'mon, the others are over at the restaurant."

James shrugged and began following her.

"And I'm sorry for how the boys behaved in the afternoon," Rachel said over her shoulder. "They're such pigs. I asked them to behave tonight. But knowing them, that may not work."

They walked over to a table where the other three were seated, munching on snacks from a nearby vending machine. Stacy wore a black jumper and beanie over her head; Nick was rugged-up with a green mountaineering jacket; while Travis was completely out of place only wearing a T-shirt and shorts.

"Hi James," Stacy said, looking up with a smile. "We were just discussing how stupid Travis is."

"Say whatever you like," Travis dismissed with a roll of his eyes. "You know I look good."

"I've always wondered what you'd look like frozen," Rachel said sarcastically.

"Ooo, *burn!*" Nick said sniggering; the others groaned at the joke.

James kept quiet, not wanting to draw attention to himself after being the butt of the boys' jokes earlier. He liked the girls. He didn't even mind Nick so much – he seemed like a jovial kid who just tried to impress both sides of the group of friends. But Travis just rubbed him the wrong way. *Yep, better to stay quiet and let them all fight it out between themselves,* he thought.

"So why are you all quiet tonight?" Travis suddenly asked him – almost like he could read his mind.

James sighed, his cover broken. He looked down at his watch and said, "Oh, I'm just wondering when the tour starts."

"Should be any minute now," Rachel said.

On cue, the woman behind the ticketing desk stood up and walked out into the foyer, clapping her hands together loudly.

"Excuse me everyone," she called out. "The eight o'clock tour will begin now. I'd like to introduce your guide for tonight, Matthew."

Out of a side door emerged a tall man wearing a long black trench coat, and a floppy black hat that covered most of his face. In his hands he carried three lanterns.

"Please follow me ... if you dare," he said in a deep, spine chilling voice.

CHAPTER FIVE

Matthew the tour guide led them down a wide path, away from the Visitor Centre and to the edge of what are called the Government Gardens. In daylight the gardens are filled with colourful flowers, but now the large gardens were shrouded in darkness.

The guide put the three lanterns down on the ground. "Gather around everyone, into a semi-circle please," he instructed.

It took a moment for the entire group to assemble.

"Good evening everyone. Once again, I'm Matthew, your ghost tour guide. Tonight we're going to roam around visiting some of the buildings all over the site."

James looked at the people around him. The group numbered around twenty-five, and was a mixture of young and old. There was a boy who looked around ten years old with his parents, but otherwise the five of them were the youngest. The oldest were an elderly couple who looked to be in their seventies.

"Before we start," Matthew continued, "I want to tell you that there are no certainties tonight. You may experience something, or you may not. But my job isn't to convince you that ghosts exist. I'm just going to tell you some stories about the site. But some of them involve people just like you; people who went on a tour and depending on how you look at it, were lucky enough – or unlucky – to experience something."

Murmurs broke out through the group. James grinned. It was everything he'd hoped for. The atmosphere was electric.

"Nothing is set up on the tour," the guide continued. "We don't have people dressed up in costumes ready to jump out from behind trees. There aren't any sound effects to spook you either. The only thing is that we've got another group thirty minutes ahead of us. So if you see three lights moving around, it's probably just them. We're also the last tour tonight, so we won't have anyone behind us. If you see or hear anything, please speak up, and maybe I'll be able to tell your story on a ghost tour in the future as well...

"Now, some of you may not really know what a ghost is. A ghost can be a dead person whose soul hasn't moved on. A lot of people think that they don't realise that they're dead. But I think that some of them know very well, and for some reason they stay here, or they're trapped."

James gulped, and around him the other kids shuffled their feet uneasily.

Matthew continued: "So why would ghosts be here? Generally, ghosts seem to be attached to places that have great meaning to them. But they're also drawn to places where they suffered enormous pain. Port Arthur fits the bill perfectly for that one. The convicts here suffered greatly in many ways. It really wasn't a nice place at all, and that's why people suggest that Port Arthur has so many ghosts."

The tour guide let the group nervously whisper to each other for a moment.

"Having a good time?" Rachel leaned over to James.

"Yeah, this is great."

Her eyes shimmered against the glow of the lanterns. "Just wait. It gets better. The stories are so cool."

The tour guide spoke up again. "Now, I'm not your babysitter. If anything happens, you're on your own. I'll be running the opposite direction *away* from the action."

The group chuckled uneasily, not liking the idea of being left alone, even if the tour guide was only joking.

"Before we get underway I need to ask for a few volunteers as well, because we need the lanterns to light our way. Firstly I need someone up the front. You need to be brave because the ghosts are going to see you first."

The group laughed nervously again.

"But at least you'll have me by your side," Matthew continued, "because I need to direct you where to go. So are there any takers?"

A man in his thirties up the front boldly put his hand up, receiving a small cheer from the group.

"Thank you sir," Matthew said, handing him a lantern. "Now the middle lantern bearer. This is the easiest job, because you'll be in the centre of the group with everyone to protect you."

Two women in their early twenties giggled and put their hands up together. "We'll share it if we can," one of them said.

"That's not a problem," Matthew said, handing them a lantern.

The group whispered again a little. The guide cleared his throat. "And that brings us to the final lantern. Personally, I'd never take this job. The person at the back is the most likely to meet a ghost. It's happened more than once on my tours."

"It *sooo* hasn't," Travis called out.

"Well, I hope for your sake that we don't test that out tonight," the guide quickly replied. Travis rolled his eyes.

But no one put their hand up this time. Travis laughed loudly.

"I can see you'll be trouble," Matthew said, suspiciously eying Travis' clothes up and down. "The ghosts love people like you. They pick on those who don't believe. Somehow they sense it."

Travis didn't look convinced.

"There's no shame in being scared," Matthew grinned under his big black hat. "I have a radio to call the Visitor Centre, and they'll drive out and pick anyone up who has enough. Once I left on a tour like this with twenty-five people, and only came back with four."

Travis groaned. "Sure, I'll do it if everyone else is too scared."

Nick sniggered and pushed him forward to collect the lantern. The group clapped.

"What's your name?" the guide asked Travis.

"James," he lied, barely holding back a laugh.

"It's actually Travis," Rachel called out.

"Yeah, it's Travis," Stacy supported. The group laughed. James looked up at the sky, begging for strength.

"Okay then, Travis. This is also the most important job, because you need to make sure that no one falls behind and gets lost. I'd also like everyone to look back occasionally and check that a ghost hasn't taken him either."

Travis laughed nervously. He didn't look quite as brave as before.

"Now, are there any questions?" the guide asked the group.

Nobody replied.

"Okay, then if we're ready, let's head off to our first stop."

Matthew spun around and started walking with the lead lantern bearer beside him; the rest of the group slowly began following. Their footsteps crunched on the gravel path and echoed around them.

James was looking around the dark garden, trying to spot a ghost. But if it was that easy, everyone would see them.

He realised that the garden must be stunning during the day. There were all sorts of flowers, and in the centre was the shadowy outline of a huge fountain, squirting water high into the air. But as he admired the gardens the thing that really struck him was the 'size' of the darkness around them. The lanterns were only little pinpricks of light. Port Arthur really is huge.

Behind him, at the very end of the group, Nick and Travis were trying to push each other off the path and into the garden.

Nick was heavier, and managed to knock Travis over. The lantern flew out of his hands and into a rose bush. Its light snuffed out.

"You're in trouble now," Travis growled at Nick.

"Oh? You're the one that's meant to be looking after it."

James and Rachel stopped together, and both pulled small pocket flashlights out of their pockets.

"You brought one too, eh?" Rachel asked.

"Always prepared," James replied.

"C'mon you idiots; hurry up out of there," Rachel demanded. "You're going to get us all into trouble. Is the lantern broken?"

Travis reached into the rose bush and jabbed his hand on a thorn. "Ouch," he yelped. He reached in again – more carefully this time – and pulled the lantern out. Amazingly it wasn't broken.

"Nah, I think that it's okay," he reported.

"Thank heavens for that," Rachel said in relief.

James almost jumped out of his skin when he turned and saw Stacy standing beside him. She'd quietly walked up to them and was almost invisible – like a ghost with her pale white skin and dark clothes.

"Let's get a move on," Stacy ordered impatiently. "Hopefully Matt the tour guide has a match to re-light it."

"Don't worry." Travis pulled out a firelighter from his pocket and relit the lantern.

"Why do you carry around a lighter?" Rachel scolded.

"You know," he shrugged in reply, "to burn ants and stuff."

"You're awful!" Stacy hissed.

"We'd better get back," James said, looking over his shoulder in worry. The tour group was now fifty metres ahead of them.

They all ran together, and reached the end of the group just as they were entering the church.

Walking in, James was shocked by how beautiful it was. A set of lights on the outside lit-up the clean stone walls with a magnificent orange light, making the building stand out brightly in the night.

It was missing its roof, long gone after a fire, and was completely empty inside. The stone floor had been removed years ago as well, and now only grass grew in its place.

Matthew waited for the group to assemble again.

"As you can guess, this is the church." He pointed to the tall stone spires and huge arches that would have once had stained glass windows.

"The church has an interesting history, drenched in blood, and not surprisingly, it is very much haunted."

James looked around. The corners were very dark, but he couldn't imagine a church being "drenched in blood". Just where he was looking in the south corner, Matthew shone a powerful torch that he pulled from his coat.

"In 1835, the foundations for the walls were being dug. In the trench a convict named Joseph was digging. Another convict, William, stood above him, and suddenly struck Joseph multiple times in the head with a pickaxe, killing him."

"Oh my God," Rachel moaned.

"Oh my God *isn't* right, young lady," the guide said. "This church was never consecrated."

"What does consecrated mean?" she whispered to James.

"I think it's when they bless a church to a certain religion."

"You're quite right," Matthew overheard James saying. "Despite being a church, this was never holy ground. Amazingly, this church could hold over a thousand people at a time. There were people of all sorts of faiths imprisoned at Port Arthur, so they didn't give it to any one religion."

For a moment the wind picked up, and the trees around the church rustled. All of the noises heightened James' senses.

"The construction of this church took one life when Joseph died and another when William was executed for his murder. But then there was another death here. The next year, in 1836, another pair of convicts were working on finishing the roof, and one of them fell, hitting his head on the wall. They'd been seen earlier having an argument, but no one came forward to say he'd been pushed."

James looked at the wall and tried to block out the nasty image from his head.

"Was it another murder? We'll probably never know for sure," the guide shook his head. "But a ghostly shadow has been seen moving around where he fell. There's also an old wives' tale that says ivy will never grow where a murdered man's blood has fallen. That's interesting, because ivy grew all over the walls after the fire that burnt the church down; everywhere *except* the spot where the man hit his head and died."

"*Eeekkkkkk!*" The entire group jumped as Stacy suddenly shrieked into the night.

"I'm going to kill you Travis!" she yelled after he put an icy hand on the back of her neck without warning.

"The church is the perfect place for it," Travis grinned back at her, proud of his handiwork.

James saw Matthew rolling his eyes, like he'd seen this sort of behaviour all before on his tours.

"We'll be moving along now," Matthew declared. He also pointed upwards, saying: "The mysterious Lady in Blue has been seen in the bell tower and reaching out towards people, but we'll talk about her later." The group all looked up, hoping to catch a glimpse of her in the haunted tower, but she couldn't be seen.

They began moving with Matthew leading the way. But then he stopped them in the edge of the church.

"I'll tell you one more ghost story here. A tour guide was once finishing up for the night. He was walking back to the Visitor Centre when he heard a sound in the corner of the church, like something falling. It was the exact spot where Joseph was killed by the pickaxe. He walked to the corner to investigate; worried that masonry from the walls might have fallen. But then something hit him in the back of the head, hard enough to knock him out.

"He woke up soon afterwards on the ground and looked around with his torch. He spent a few minutes trying to find something – *anything* – that could have hit him, but there was nothing at all on the ground."

The group looked shocked at the story.

"I don't want to alarm you," Matthew said in a low voice, and choosing his words carefully, "because the tours are meant to be about having fun. But some of the ghosts here are dangerous, and given the opportunity they can hurt you."

Fiddling with his torch, James heard the dire warning but dismissed it with a laugh, grinning bravely at Rachel.

His grin wouldn't last long.

CHAPTER SIX

The tour group turned left from the church and began walking back past the Government Gardens. A few people whispered to each other, but most looked around at the darkness, hoping to catch a glimpse or hear something.

After the guide's warning, for now at least, Nick and Travis were strangely silent as well. But James was more excited than ever – treating it like a game. He swung his head side to side, searching for movement in the gloom.

The group followed the guide's lead, and a few minutes later they walked past Mason Cove along the waterfront, and also saw the huge shadowy outline of the Penitentiary building, where most of the convicts had been housed.

"I really hope that we go in there as well," James said to Rachel as they walked alongside each other.

A minute later they arrived at the Guard Tower, a building used to keep a look-out over the prison site.

But instead of taking them to the top of the tower, Matthew the guide led them to the bottom, and inside a room dug into the side of the hill.

When everyone was inside, Matthew closed the heavy wooden door behind them with a thud that echoed around in the small space. The room was circular, around five metres in diameter with a stone floor and walls.

"This, to me personally, is one of the most unsettling buildings on the site," the guide began. "It really is a sad room with an unfortunate past." He stepped into the centre of the room. "The Guard Tower was built in 1835, just like the church. It was built to keep an eye on the prisoners from a slightly higher vantage point. I love its design; I really think it's beautiful. But all isn't as it seems."

James shifted his weight, leaning against the wall as he listened.

"Originally this room was used to store ammunition and weapons. But they soon found that it was too damp to keep gun power in, so they converted it, and it became the 'condemned cell'. At the church you heard about how prisoners could be executed – given a death sentence for awful crimes they committed while they were here. Remember, Port Arthur was where the worst of the worst were kept – repeat offenders. Some continued their ways, and there were a few prisoners sentenced to death for killing each other. However, the executions weren't carried out here, but at Hobart."

Matthew the guide looked at everyone cramped into the small round room.

"So can anyone guess where they were kept before they were transported?" He grinned seeing everyone's wide-eyed reactions. "Yep, in this room."

James pushed himself away from the wall. He remembered what Matthew said about ghosts being drawn to places where they suffered. He could easily imagine that this was one of those places. But he had no idea just how bad it would have been to be kept here, knowing you were going to die soon.

"Only a few years after the tower was built," Matthew continued, "a convict lad named Henry went into the woods with his friend called Thomas. But when he returned, he was alone. Henry told the officials that Thomas had run away, and search parties were sent out to capture him. Four days later, Thomas was found with a knife stuck in his neck. Amazingly, he was still alive, but he was an inch away from death.

"Thomas lived long enough to tell the Commandant in charge that Henry attacked him. When Thomas died Henry was sentenced to death, and was kept in this room for fifteen days waiting for transport to arrive. There used to be plenty of boats in the harbour, but only the bravest captains would take condemned criminals, because they were considered to be bad luck."

Stacy and Rachel held onto each other's arms, and when Travis saw them he started to shake and pulled a crying face. "Babies," he whispered to them.

Matthew looked at Travis in disapproval, but continued the story. "The wait would be awful for any person, but the soldiers were on the level right above Henry, and they teased him mercilessly through cracks in the wooden floor; telling him how his neck was going to snap when he was hung. Henry kept screaming and screaming for two whole weeks until he was transported away. To this day you can still hear the sounds of a boy screaming from this cell, and some people see him sitting in the back of the cell – right where you're standing," he pointed to Rachel.

She shrieked and jumped aside. The entire group laughed at her – none more than Travis and Nick, who both copied her and jumped aside.

Matthew moved towards the door, and opened it with a loud creak that reminded James of fingernails down a blackboard. "Now we'll be going to the Surgeon's House."

The group began filing out, and as they walked past, James overheard the elderly couple complaining about Travis' behaviour. James waited until everyone else was gone, and walked with the other kids at the back of the group.

"I think you should tone it down a bit," James said to Travis as they followed the tour down Champ Street. "I heard some of the other people complaining."

Travis laughed at him. "Are you serious? What are you going to do about it? Tell on me to the tour guide? Grow up."

"You grow up," Rachel said. "I asked you to behave before the tour started, and instead you're being a total pig."

Travis snorted. "Yeah, and what do you think Nick?"

Stacy answered before Nick had a chance: "You're both being idiots. Just because you're freezing your butt off doesn't mean you have to take it out on all the other people on the tour."

"Whatever," Travis replied. Nick walked on in silence, his feelings hurt.

Suddenly James stopped dead in his tracks.

"Did you see that?" he exclaimed with surprise.

"What?" They all stopped and looked to him.

"Over there, in the field. There was a flash of light. Look! It just happened again." They all turned to where he was eagerly pointing.

"There's nothing there," Travis dismissed.

"It was an intense white light, above the ground. It just flashed for a moment both times," James insisted.

"Could be someone playing a prank?" Nick asked seriously.

"Nah, Travis is here with us," Stacy said rolling her eyes.

"It wasn't a person," James insisted. "Can you see anyone out there? I can't."

"It could've been the other tour group," Rachel said. "Remember? Matthew said they're ahead of us. Over there is where they'll be walking next."

"It wasn't a tour group," James mumbled. "They wouldn't just disappear."

They stood in silence for a few seconds, waiting for the light to appear again, but it didn't.

"I swear I saw a light," James sighed, certain his eyes weren't playing tricks on him. "C'mon, we need to get moving," he finally said in frustration.

In their rush to catch up to the tour group, none of them saw the light blink again behind them.

CHAPTER SEVEN

The group took a path to the Magistrate's and Surgeon's House that led them alongside a small garden. As they arrived the guide instructed the first two lantern bearers to leave their lanterns outside before the group would go down another set of stairs – leading underneath the stone house.

By arriving last, the kids at the back of the group were actually in a position to be the first to enter. Following the guide and Stacy, James was the third person to walk down the stairs. But something wasn't right.

Immediately at the bottom of the stairs his nose and throat began burning with the most awful smell he'd ever experienced. The sharp odour left him choking and gagging for air.

Matthew the guide spun around in concern. "What's the matter?" he asked. Behind them, the rest of the tour group came to a sharp halt on the stairs.

"There's a terrible smell down here," James said in a raspy voice.

"I don't smell anything," Stacy replied.

"*You* don't have to smell anything for *him* to smell something," Matthew said in concern. "What does it smell like?"

"It's some sort of chemical; I can't describe it. It's burning my nose and throat."

"Okay," Matthew nodded. "Clear a path!" he yelled to the group walking down the stairs. Everyone squeezed against the wall to let them pass. Matthew led James back up the stairs as he coughed, and sat him down against a low wall. "How is it now? Can you breathe now?"

"Yes," James replied with a single nod, sucking down air.

"You don't have to go down there," Matthew explained. "You can wait out here, but it would be best if someone else stayed with you."

"I'll do it," Rachel volunteered – she'd followed them back up as well.

"Okay, good," Matthew said. "We won't be long down there. When I get back, I'll explain what happened to you."

James nodded without saying anything, and Matthew raced back down the uneven stairs to the waiting group to continue the next stop of their tour.

Travis appeared from the back of the group. "You okay princess?" he asked, fluttering his eyelids. "You're even worse at trying to get attention than I am! First you say you see a light no one else sees, and then you smell something that no one else can."

"I didn't make any of it up," James said, shocked that he was being called a liar.

"Yeah, sure, whatever you say, drama queen." Travis glanced at Rachel, adding, "I said he was too chicken for this, didn't I?" He quickly spun around, and raced back after the group, leaving James and Rachel alone.

Turning to Rachel, James felt devastated. His dream trip to Port Arthur was being ruined just like the rest of his holiday.

"You believe me, don't you?" he said, looking pleadingly into her eyes.

"You're a nice person," she said. "If you say it happened, then it did. I guess I've smelled stuff before that others couldn't."

"It was just so powerful," he thought aloud. "I don't know how no one else could smell it."

She didn't reply at first.

"I shouldn't have come on the tour," he continued sulking beside her while she stared off into the distance.

"Can I tell you a secret?" Rachel finally said. "When I walked down the stairs ... I'm not sure, but I think I started to smell the same thing."

"It's sweet of you to try," James sighed, "but you don't need to lie to make me feel better."

"I'm not ly—"

35

"Just forget about it," he shook his head.

They sat in silence until the group reappeared. At least they had the gentle glow of the lanterns to make them feel safe.

Finally people started emerging from the basement.

Once again Matthew waited for the group to assemble before he announced that they would go to the Accountant's House next. When the group got moving he motioned to James to walk with him at the front, and Rachel followed close behind.

"Are you feeling better?" Matthew asked. James nodded. "I'm glad to hear it. What you experienced is something that a lot of other people have before, and a mystery surrounds it. Down those stairs was a morgue – where they kept dead bodies, and also what is called the dissection room. What you smelled is a chemical called formaldehyde."

"So I wasn't imagining it?" James said in relief.

"Hardly," Matthew shook his head. "Quite a few doctors that go down there have smelled it as well. Formaldehyde is used in the preparation of dead bodies. Certain 'sensitive' people – usually those working with people or animals, have experienced it just like you did. But when you aren't used to the smell, it can be really overpowering."

"I believed you," Rachel said reassuringly with a tender smile.

"The thing is," Matthew continued, "formaldehyde wasn't used until after Port Arthur closed. So we don't know why some people smell it here. That's where the mystery comes in. We just can't explain why it happens."

Behind them a cry rang out into the night, and then sounds of a scuffle.

"It's okay, it's just those stupid kids," one of the people on the tour said irritably. The entire group stopped for a second to see what was happening.

Matthew shook his head. "Friends of yours?" he asked James.

"Not really. I'm just visiting from Brisbane."

"Technically they're my friends," Rachel admitted. "I'm sorry. They're just a pair of baboons."

"It's not your fault," Matthew consoled. "But they're really slowing us down. At this rate we'll have to miss one of the planned stops on the tour," he said regretfully.

The group continued walking until they reached the Accountant's House; a simple single-storey house painted in white.

James and Rachel stood apart from Stacy, Nick and Travis. Matthew began talking as soon as everyone settled in front of the building. "Well, there are a few ghosts floating around this house, including the Lady in Blue, who I mentioned earlier at the church."

"Floating around?" Travis asked. Some people groaned, expecting some wisecrack. "Like Jasper the friendly ghost?"

"That's *Casper* the friendly ghost," James corrected. The entire group laughed at the troublemaker's expense.

Travis made a throat cutting gesture with his hand. "You're dead," Travis mouthed at James. Rachel saw all of it.

"As I was saying," Matthew resumed, "there are many ghosts around this house..."

Rachel tugged on James' jacket and pulled him aside from the circle of people carefully listening to the tour guide.

"Travis just makes me sick," she said.

James didn't reply.

"I can see in your eyes that you agree."

"So what if I do?" James said crossly.

"Want to really get back at him and Nick for being total thugs, and humiliate them in front of everyone else?"

"Maybe," he replied, knowing it was wrong, but still desperately wanting to get back at them. "Why? What have you got in mind?"

"Something devious." Her white teeth shone in the passing moonlight as she grinned. "The tour is going to the Parsonage next. It has to. It's one of the coolest houses on the entire site, and it's just next door from here."

"Yeah, and?"

"We hide inside, and then when those two come in we jump out and scare the living daylights out of them!"

"I don't know..."

"Aww, c'mon," Rachel urged him. "It'll be hysterical. And you'll also be getting them back for the water thing before."

James remembered all too well; the memory of his soaked shirt in front of Rachel and how embarrassed he'd been.

"Okay," he said finally, nodding his head. "Let's do it."

"You won't regret it," she giggled. "Follow me. The Parsonage isn't far away from here at all."

They silently snuck away and tip-toed off into the night, completely unseen by anyone from the tour group.

But one pair of eyes outside of the group took careful note of which way they were going.

CHAPTER EIGHT

The Parsonage is a simple two-storey brick house with a steeped corrugated iron roof. Yet in daytime the house is strangely ominous – a sense of unease entering those who dare trespass. At night though, the house takes on a life of its own.

James and Rachel hesitated as they approached, having to open a small white gate at the bottom of the garden.

They walked up the paved path and onto a narrow wooden porch. The front door groaned when James pushed it open.

"Well, at least we'll hear them when they come in," James commented dryly. He shut the door behind him with an equally loud protest.

They both reached into their pockets and fished out their small flashlights.

"This place smells old," James said, wrinkling his nose.

He'd brought the 'Convict Trail' information brochure with him, and fishing it out of his pocket turned to a page on the Parsonage. He read that it was built in 1842, and after being damaged by bushfires in 1895 it was rebuilt to be a post office.

"Okay, we need to find places to hide," Rachel said, looking around the entryway for a spot. "The last time I was here there was a chest and a large cabinet in the side room. They'd be perfect to jump out from."

As they walked into the first room on the left, a floorboard creaked, sending shivers down James' spine. "Not only does it smell old, it's creeping me out."

Sure enough, a large chest sat beside the wall of the room. Rachel swung her torch around the room, but they couldn't see the cabinet.

"Oh no, they must have moved it since I was here last. It must be in one of the other rooms."

They moved through the four other rooms on the bottom floor, but couldn't find any trace of the cabinet. The stairs to the top floor of the house were barred-off, so there was no other way up there.

"Well, what are we going to do now?" James asked. "That chest isn't large enough to fit both of us inside."

"No, but I saw another spot that will do just as well. Follow me."

Rachel led him to a room at the back of the house, and she walked over to a fireplace. Beside the fireplace was a pair of wide, deep holes in the brick wall for storing firewood. They were pitch black inside.

"I can slither in there," she exclaimed. "I'll have to go in legs first, but I'll just be able to fit."

James looked horrified at the thought. "Won't you be scared in that cramped hole all alone?" he asked.

"Are you kidding me? You don't really believe in ghosts, do you?"

James hesitated answering. "I don't know..."

"Well I don't," she said firmly. She tugged at his jacket and pointed to the other room. "C'mon; they'll be here soon. Go to the chest, climb in, and when you hear them come into the room, jump out and go nuts."

"And you'll be fine?"

"Yes," she rolled her eyes. "Please James, just go."

"When I know you're okay..."

"And they say chivalry is dead," she joked.

Rachel dropped to the ground, and shimmied herself into the firewood hole like a reversing snake. She was just small enough to entirely fit into the gap without poking out.

"Satisfied?" she asked when she was all the way in.

"Yes," he replied.

She turned her flashlight off, signalling James to go to his hiding spot.

His shoes banged loudly on the floorboards; the sound echoing throughout the house. *I'd hate to live here*, he thought.

When he made it to the front room he carefully climbed into the large wooden chest on the floor. It was just big enough for him to fit into if he lay on his back, pushed his knees up, and tucked his head in.

With a small squeak he dropped the lid down and suddenly felt very alone. He immediately felt claustrophobic in the small, dark space, and turned his torch on. The inside of the chest lit up, and on the top of the lid he could see a small carving saying: "Made in 1871". After all these years the chest still smelled of pine.

Any minute now, he thought to himself, checking his watch for the time. He began tapping a beat on the side of the chest with his fingers, but then stopped almost as quickly as he began – wanting to hear any sounds outside.

He sat silently for a couple of minutes, but with nothing happening, and his unease dropping, he decided to turn the torch off and save the batteries.

"You're in a chest; nothing is going to come inside and get you," he tried to reassure himself in the darkness. "Rachel's right. There's no such thing as ghosts." He'd never had a ghost encounter before, so surely she was right, wasn't she?

But he suddenly thought back to the start of the day, when he'd visited the Officers' Quarters at Eaglehawk Neck. What had touched him in that dark room; and why had he felt so scared just before it happened? Had he sensed something – someone – in the room with him?

What about the light in the field as they were walking to the Surgeon's House? He'd seen it flash – twice – in the middle of an empty field. Maybe it was only a bit of glass sitting on the ground, with moonlight reflecting off it as clouds passed by?

But that still left the question of the smell. He had no idea what to think of the putrid fumes in the basement. Had the guide just made up the story about the chemical smell and 'sensitive people' being able to detect it to make him feel better?

Maybe he'd only been jumpy in the Officer's Quarters, and maybe he'd imagined the light. But the smell at least had been real. Even now his nose still tingled from the effects of it.

"But that wasn't really ghosts, was it?" he murmured to himself. "It was just a smell... A smell can't be a ghost, can it?"

Settling back, he cleared his mind and concentrated on listening for sounds. He was in the room at the front of the house, so he'd be able to hear people walking across the porch before they opened the noisy front door – which he would definitely hear. It really was the perfect position for their prank.

With his concentration amplified in the dark he almost entered a trance-like state, where he focused solely on the sound of nothing.

CHAPTER NINE

Matthew the guide and the tour group stood outside the Accountant's House. The group was growing increasingly angry.

Travis and Nick had constantly interrupted the story at the building. Even worse, now they were having a mock fight, swinging their arms around like windmills. Other people on the tour had to scamper out of their way to avoid being hit.

"Okay, that's it," Matthew said loudly and briskly walked over to both of them; grabbing their arms mid-swing and dragging them to the side.

"Do you want me to call over a car and have you ejected off the tour? Better yet, I can have you banned from here for life. You've disrupted the tour the entire night, and everyone is disgusted with your behaviour."

Stacy stood away from the pair in silence, not wanting to be associated with them in front of the others on the tour. Frowning, she glanced around looking for Rachel and James, but couldn't see them anywhere.

"We're really sorry," Nick said, lowering his head guiltily.

"Oh, is that so?" Matthew asked. "Because this is your last chance boys. I hate to punish everyone because of the actions of two fools, but because of you we're so far behind time that we're going to have to miss going to the Parsonage, and that's really a huge shame."

"Why's that?" Travis asked.

Matthew looked him square in the eyes. "Because it's one of the two most haunted houses in Australia. I've had more things happen on tours in that house than anywhere else. But it's your own fault we aren't going."

Looks of disappointment flashed across both the boy's faces.

Matthew turned around and addressed the waiting group.

"I'm really sorry for all of the interruptions, but I think they've sorted themselves out now," he said with a smile. "We'll now be going on to our second last stop of the night – the haunted Penitentiary."

CHAPTER TEN

The wait felt like hours, but when James finally had enough and turned his torch on to look at his watch, he saw that it had only been seventeen minutes since he'd climbed into the chest.

"What's taking them so long?" he grumbled in frustration.

He decided to wait three more minutes to make it an even twenty before giving up and going to Rachel. In the meantime, he thought about what had gone wrong.

Had they seen them sneak off? No, that didn't make sense; even if they did the tour would come there anyway. Maybe Rachel was wrong? Matthew had never said they were coming to the Parsonage. Maybe she'd just wrongly assumed that because she'd been on a tour that had gone there before. Then he remembered that Matthew the guide said that they were behind time and might need to skip a stop. Could that be it?

But then an even worse thought came to him.

What if he'd been set-up? What if this was all a cruel joke at his expense and Rachel had lured him out to the house while they were all laughing at him outside? He remembered back to when they'd first met and Travis pulled his hand back. She'd laughed for a moment as well... And after all, they were lifelong friends and he was the outsider. The thought made his stomach turn.

He flicked his flashlight on again and glanced at his watch. Twenty-one minutes since he'd climbed into the chest.

"Oh stuff it," he muttered. His neck had become far too sore, and it was painfully clear now that the tour group wasn't coming to the Parsonage.

The lid groaned as he lifted it and he stood up; stretching his arms and legs, and savouring being able to roll his head around. He let off a satisfied *ahhh* before closing the chest.

Turning around and flashing his torch towards the door, he almost yelped when he saw a man standing there.

"Holy–Oh my God. You scared the bejesus out of me."

"I'm so sorry," the man quickly replied, seeming almost as surprised as James. Standing in the doorway, he was fairly short – around James' height, but he was about thirty years old, with black hair and a very square jaw.

"H-Holy cow," James stammered. He'd never been more frightened in his entire life. His heart was pounding against his chest like a freight train.

"Again, I'm sorry," the man said with a soft English accent. Though his jaw was distinctive, the man's most remarkable feature was his incredibly sad dark brown eyes. They almost pleaded James for forgiveness.

"It's okay," James assured, although he was sure he'd just taken away a few years from his life.

For a moment the two stood staring at each other. The man was wearing a plain white buttoned-up shirt, and brown trousers with polished black shoes. James tried to remember him from the tour, but he was sure that he didn't recognise him.

"You weren't in the group, were you?" James asked.

"No, I wasn't," he replied with a shake of his head.

"Then who are you?"

The man smiled, nodding towards James. "My name is Thomas Burke. But please, call me Tom."

"Pleased to meet you, Tom. I'm James Masters."

The man didn't step forward to shake hands, and James stayed standing where he was in the middle of the room.

"So, umm, if you don't mind me asking, what are you doing here?" James inquired.

Tom stood still for a moment, contemplating the question. "I'm a sort of caretaker here; following people around and looking after things," he replied, and only now stepped closer to James. "Do you mind if I ask what you're doing here, and hiding in that chest?"

"You aren't going to arrest me or something for being in here, are you?" James cautiously asked.

"Heavens no," Tom replied with a smile.

"Well, in that case, I guess there's no harm in telling you that I was hiding in there to scare some kids I met."

"It is a good place for it," Tom agreed with a nod.

"But it didn't exactly go according to plan," James admitted. He then tilted his head questioningly. "Say, how did you get in here without me hearing you?"

Tom chuckled and shook his head. "When you have been around here as long as I have, you get to learn every bump and groan that an old haunted building makes. I have become pretty good at sneaking around unseen and unheard." Tom looked around the room, and motioned with his hand to the chest. "You know," he began, "this house wasn't always like this."

"Yeah," James said. "She said that the furniture got moved around."

"She?" Tom looked confused for a moment. "Oh. You must mean the girl hiding in the firewood chute."

James' expression showed a mixture of surprise and being impressed. "How did you know she's in there?"

"I saw her, of course." Tom took another step towards James, and now stood only a metre away.

"Then how come she isn't with you now?"

"I'm afraid that I don't understand the question," Tom replied.

"It is pitch dark in there. If you saw her, then she would have seen you – in which case she would've spoken to you, and she would have come out."

Tom laughed softly. "But she didn't see me. Not too many people do."

James pursed his lips, wondering what he meant by that. He briefly moved the beam of the torch over Tom. Something didn't seem normal about him. Was it just a case of "stranger danger"? The hair on the back of his neck pricked up, and he suddenly realised how cold the room had become. *Was it this cold earlier?* he wondered.

"That isn't original," Tom said suddenly, pointing again at the chest, "The last family that lived here bought it, and then left it here. They were in a rush to leave this house. I have heard some people say that this is one of the most haunted houses in Australia."

James' companion smiled again, and let off a long sigh. A second later, instead of feeling warmth, a rush of ice-cold air ran past James' face. Just as it had in the Officer's Quarters at Eaglehawk Neck.

Oh my God.

James took a step back, and then another, but his heel got caught on the chest. He tripped backwards in fright and fell against the wall – over the chest. The weight of his body pressing against it caused the chest to slide forward along the smooth wooden floor.

James fell painfully to the ground – the chest no longer under his backside. His unsupported legs then pushed the chest even further along the floor. Looking up, James could see it standing in the middle of the room.

For a fraction of a second his heart stopped.

Looking up higher, he could see Thomas Burke standing unmoved in the centre of the room. Half of his legs were hidden by the chest. But from his position sprawled on the ground, James could also see Tom's feet.

But Tom wasn't standing behind the chest. Was he standing in it? No, the lid was closed – he was standing *through it.* Through *solid wood!*

James made a gagging sound like he was choking. But instead he was just taking a massive breath. A moment later his screams tore through the haunted house.

CHAPTER ELEVEN

Hearing James screaming from the other side of the house, Rachel scampered out of her hole, and only a second later she was in the room.

When she ran in all that she could see was the chest in the middle of the room and James sprawled on the ground. He looked pale enough like he'd seen a ghost.

"James," she exclaimed in worry. "Are you alright? Did you fall over the chest?"

It took him half a minute to reply. He kept glancing between her and the chest – his mouth wide open.

"James? James – are you alright? Did you hit your head?"

...

James was hyperventilating, taking one rapid breath after another.

Tom was still standing there with his legs through the chest, and Rachel wasn't doing anything. She should've been running out of the house with her arms in the air screaming. *No, I should be running out of the house screaming!* James thought in panic. But he was too paralysed with fear to even move a muscle.

She repeated his name, and that almost sent him back to earth.

"Y-Y-You don't see him, do you?" His mouth quivered and body began shaking.

"See who? You hit your head against the wall, didn't you?" she said with a frown.

Tom stepped through the chest, and moved to stand beside Rachel. "She can't see me, James. See?" the ghost waved his hand in front of her.

"Why?" James asked.

Rachel put her hand to her forehead in concern. "Why what?"

But Tom answered his question instead. "Some special people can see us, James. Very few actually. When I saw that you could see me I was almost as surprised as you were." He sighed deeply as he had before.

Rachel suddenly shivered. "Who turned up the air con? It's freezing in here."

Tom looked at her quizzically. "That's strange. She can clearly sense my presence, but can't see me or hear me."

James closed his eyes as tightly as he could for two seconds, hoping everything would be gone when he opened them. But he jumped clear off the ground in fright when he opened them again – Rachel had moved and was leaning directly over him.

"Oh my God, Rachel. Tell me you can see him. Please, I'm begging you. Please!"

The concern for him vanished from her face. Instead she looked frightened and worried about herself. "I'm getting a bit scared, James... You're acting very strangely."

He reached up and grabbed her fluffy pink jacket tightly. He immediately released his grip when he realised he was scaring her even more.

"I think you need to calm down," Tom said in a soothing voice. "I don't know exactly what is going on. But clearly you don't see ghosts every day, or you wouldn't be reacting like this. I am not going to harm you. I did not mean to scare you..."

James looked into Rachel's green eyes. "Promise me just one thing."

"... Okay..." she hesitated. His behaviour was beyond alarming. She thought that she should never have suggested them coming to the Parsonage.

James sat up. He suspiciously eyed the centre of the room where Tom was standing.

"Stand over there," James directed to Tom – pointing to the back of the room. Rachel began to move "–No, not you," he said shaking his head. She backed away carefully towards the door instead.

"Rachel, I know you aren't going to believe this, but you've got to promise to listen to me. Can you please do that? Just hear me out, and then you never have to see me again. I'll just disappear back to Brisbane, and you'll soon forget this ever happened."

"Okay..." she said even more carefully than before.

"I was in the chest, and nothing happened. But when I got out, there was a man standing there without me hearing him come in. *That* man." He pointed to Tom, but Rachel only saw empty air.

"I got scared, and I tripped over the chest, and it slid *through* him. I screamed. That's when you came in. But he's still here, and he's still talking to me."

Rachel had a blank look on her face.

"You don't believe me, do you?"

She didn't reply.

James looked at Tom in despair. "You say you don't want to harm me. Then can you help me?"

"How?" Tom asked.

"Can you move something? Make something float?" James asked hopefully.

"I'm not that kind of spirit... I don't have those powers."

James sat quietly for a moment, deep in thought. Finally he thought of something. "Then do the breathing thing again – on her. Once from one side, and then from the other. You can't have drafts come from different sides at once."

"Okay," Tom agreed.

"Wait! What?" Rachel said in alarm. "What are you talking about?"

"Rachel, please just stand there," James asked.

He watched as Tom moved across to her. Walking just like a normal person, he looked completely solid – not like a ghost 'should'. Sure, he looked a bit pale, but this was Tasmania; from what James had seen sun wasn't really their thing.

When Tom was in position, James told her what was going to happen. "I'm going to cover my mouth and nose to prove it isn't me. But you're going to feel two cold breaths of air from opposite sides..."

He covered his mouth and nose, and a second later Rachel jumped.

"What was that?" she shrieked.

"... That was Tom."

"No way. No freaking way. It's just drafts. It's an old house. *No freaking way.*" She walked around the walls searching for cracks.

James felt hurt... She didn't believe him. How could he convince her?

"Rachel, do you mind if I talk to Tom a little? We need to find out a way to convince you..."

"You and the little voice in your head are craaazy," she accused. "You need serious help."

"Rachel, if you're scared of me, fine. But I'm not going to move from this spot, so I hope you stay."

She crossed her arms and didn't respond. She just scanned the room, hoping for a sign that James wasn't due for a spell in a mental institution.

"Tom, help me, please," James begged the ghost. "How come I can see you now when I couldn't before?"

"Well, it's true that you didn't see me. I was walking behind you two when you separated from the group. I wanted to see what you were doing, but you didn't see me at all until you got out of the chest."

"What's so special about the chest?" he asked the ghost.

"Nothing that I know of. It's been here for years, and it's done nothing in the past."

"Hmm," James pondered.

"What did you do in the chest?" Tom asked.

"I had the flashlight on for a little while, but then I turned it off and just sat in the dark, concentrating on hearing the others coming."

"What were you thinking about?"

"Like I said: nothing. I just concentrated really hard on hearing a sound. But I heard nothing, and I thought about nothing. I concentrated on the sound of ... nothing"

"Then maybe that is the key?" Tom suggested. "If she does what you did, then perhaps she will be able to see me as well."

"I suppose it's worth a shot," James said, and then turned to Rachel's side of the room. She'd been trying to understand the one half of the conversation she could hear. "Rachel? Would you like to try to see Tom?"

She didn't look impressed by the suggestion. "How?"

"Climb into the chest, close it, and clear your mind – focusing on trying to hear a sound for about fifteen minutes."

"Climb into a chest and close it with a potential whacko jumping around outside, locking me in? No thanks."

James didn't feel as hurt this time. He realised that if he was in her position he wouldn't believe it either.

"Then do it out of the chest. Sit down on the floor, turn off your torch, close your eyes, and concentrate. I'll sit in the far corner, and if you hear me move, you can turn your torch on and run out screaming 'Psycho! Psycho!'"

Rachel smiled for the first time since she'd run into the room. "Okay, I can try that."

She sat down on the floor with her back to the wall, and then turned off her torch. James turned his off as well, plunging the room into darkness.

Ten minutes later, after complete silence from all three of them, Tom spoke.

"Can you hear me?" he whispered from the other side of the room.

"James, I thought you wanted total silence," Rachel said angrily.

In the darkness James grinned. "Rachel ... that wasn't me."

"I swear James, if this is just you throwing your voice or something, I'll kill you."

A moment later Rachel's flashlight sparked to life. A look of total horror crossed her face.

James was sitting in the far corner – just as he had been before, cross-legged, and looking very pleased with himself.

But standing next to him was a man.

She fainted.

CHAPTER TWELVE

James tried everything he could to rouse Rachel. He tried gently slapping her cheeks, shaking her, and talking loudly at her, but nothing worked.

"The worst thing would be if she wakes up and can't see you again," he commented to Tom.

"That would be most unfortunate," the ghost replied.

They had to wait five minutes before she began coming around.

"I think it would be best if you hid for a little while, so you don't scare her again right away," James directed. Tom nodded, and literally vanished into thin air.

Rachel's green eyes fluttered open and James kneeled beside her. "Are you okay?"

"Are you?" she replied.

He grinned at her. "Never been better. Do you remember what happened?"

She groaned. "A bad nightmare."

"No, seriously," he insisted. "You saw him?"

"Yes... Oh God James, I'm sorry I ever doubted you. It's just so..."

"... Unbelievable, I know," he finished. "Would you like to see him again?"

"Do we have to?" she moaned.

"No," he said sincerely. "But isn't this incredible? Seeing and talking to an actual ghost."

Rachel bit her upper lip in thought. "I guess it is pretty special. But why do you want to talk to him again?"

"I don't know; ask him why he's here? What's it like to be dead? What happened to him? He's like a living time capsule. Okay, not 'living' – but you get my point."

Rachel threw her arms up in defeat. "Alright, let's see what's behind door number one." She braced herself against the wall.

James grinned. "Tom? Are you here Tom?"

The ghost reappeared as suddenly as he'd gone, materialising right in the middle of the room. "Greetings Rachel," he spoke.

"Oh my God, I'm talking to a ghost," she said, looking like she was about to faint again.

"Rachel! Stay with us," James said in alarm.

"I can leave if—" Tom began.

"No," she said firmly with renewed courage. "It's okay. I can see why you freaked out before."

James blushed in reply, embarrassed by how he'd acted. Though, in his defence, unlike Rachel he hadn't had any warning that he was about to meet a ghost. He screamed like a little wuss; she fainted like one. They were about even, really.

"So, umm, how do you do?" she asked.

"I am honoured to meet such a beautiful young lady," Tom replied.

Now it was Rachel's turn to blush.

"It truly is remarkable that both of you can see me and talk to me," Tom said. "As I was telling James before, very few people can see us, let alone interact with us and communicate. You are both very special."

The two of them looked at each other and grinned. Tom was a big change from the kinds of nasty ghosts they'd seen in movies.

Tom looked down for a moment and his eyes looked even sadder than they were normally. He appeared torn between something.

"You are a gift from heaven you two are. I know that this is an awful lot to ask of you, and I will understand if you say no. But although I am still here in this world, there are limitations on what I can do. Some ghosts can do different things, like move objects. But I cannot. You being here is an opportunity too good to waste. I need help, and you could be the ones to provide it. Please – can we go outside and talk about it?"

James and Rachel looked at each other apprehensively, unsure about what to do.

Obviously Tom read their expressions, saying, "I know under the circumstances ... with me being ... what I am ... changes things. So I will let you discuss it together."

Before either of them could say anything, the ghost of Thomas Burke vanished again, leaving them alone.

Rachel's eyes widened and she mouthed "wow."

"Yeah," James laughed. "It's a bit like that. So what do you want to do?"

"I don't know."

They sat in silence for a few moments, thinking about the possibilities.

"Well," she spoke up, "he said he wants to talk outside, and we need to get out of this creepy old house at some point. So how about we just hear him out? Don't commit to anything – just listen to what he wants."

James nodded. "I guess just listening won't hurt... Tom?"

The ghost reappeared in the same spot, smiling.

"You were listening, weren't you?" Rachel accused.

They saw the ghost's pale cheeks turn a slightly pink colour. "So you've made a decision?" he said innocently.

"You know we have," she teased. "You didn't leave at all. You just made yourself invisible."

"Being a ghost certainly does have its advantages," James commented.

"I apologise," Tom said with apparent sincerity. "But a lot depends on your decision. I had to know what you were deciding. I am sorry for deceiving you..."

"It's okay I guess," Rachel said looking at James – who nodded. "We're willing to listen to what you have to say."

Relief crossed Tom's face, and if it was possible James thought for a moment that the ghost was going to cry with joy. "In that case," he said softly, "could you please follow me?"

The two kids stood up and followed Tom out into the hallway and towards the front door. James was about to speak when in the corner of his eye he noticed a shadow moving on the stairs beside them.

He looked across and suddenly gripped Rachel's jacket in absolute terror.

Looming directly over them stood a giant in black, blaring his teeth.

CHAPTER THIRTEEN

The man on the stairs was huge! Looking like he was in his early fifties, he was close to two metres tall and was dressed entirely in black. He snarled at them – showing yellowed teeth, and his unkempt hair – like he'd just got out of bed; giving them a menacing, terrorising look.

"What are you doing in my house?" the man boomed down at them.

"Leave them be, Reverend," Tom defended in a low voice. It was then that James noticed that the huge man had a little white collar around his neck – worn by members of the church. "They are innocents," Tom continued. "There is no need for your conduct around them."

"There are no innocents in this devilish place," the Reverend hissed down at them. "You wish to visit Hell? Hell has come to you!"

"Come children, there is no need for you to be around him." Tom quickly ushered them to the front door and they made a hasty exit, with James quickly closing it behind them.

They hurried down the path to the gate. "That guy is terrifying," Rachel said.

"In life as in death," the ghost commented.

"Who is he?" James asked as they reached the gate. He turned around to close it behind them, but made the mistake of looking back at the house.

The Reverend was staring at him through the window of the room he'd been in with the chest. James quickly looked away, vowing to never return to the Parsonage.

"The Reverend was not a bad man by any means; he was largely misunderstood," Tom explained. "But he had a temper at times. And you saw how big he was. He towered above everyone else at the time. Naturally, people found that rather intimidating. However, I am afraid that ever since he died his temper has become much worse."

"Dying would make anyone cranky," James said.

"Indeed," Tom replied, leading them to the road in front of the haunted house. "But unlike most, he has not accepted his death, and that is part of the reason why he is still here. Worse still, like many ghosts he haunts a place he thinks is his and his alone. I have tried talking to him, but he refuses to listen. He has ... how should I put it ... a one-track mind? I fear that he will stay at the Parsonage for as long as it stands, and continue to haunt those who intrude."

They now stood out onto the gravel road in front of the Parsonage. The night had become very overcast and dark. There was a non-stop breeze gliding past their legs. "So you wanted to talk?" Rachel said.

"Yes," Tom nodded. "Let us go to St David's Church. We can speak there – no ghosts haunt it." He pointed to their left, and to a building about thirty metres away.

St David's Church was only a single-storey wooden building. Stepping inside, it was simply decorated, with red carpet, five rows of pews to sit on, and a small lectern where the minister conducts his sermons. Unlike other buildings on the Port Arthur site, St David's – built in 1927, fifty years after the prison closed down – is still used as intended to this day.

Thankfully this building had electricity, so James turned on a small overhead light, allowing them to see properly. Tom asked them to sit down, so James and Rachel sat down next to each other in the front row of pews. Tom walked around to stand behind the pulpit where the priest usually stands.

"Firstly, I would like to begin by saying thank you for agreeing to talk to me," Tom began formally. "I'm certain you have many questions, but I would like to start by telling you what I have in mind."

James and Rachel smiled for him to continue, but both were still shocked by what was happening to them.

"You met the Reverend just now. But there are others like him here at Port Arthur; people who are stuck here for various reasons. One question you both surely have is why I am still here." The pair both nodded their heads eagerly. "Unlike many others here, I had the option to leave. But I did not because I wanted to help those that have not passed over. Thankfully over the years I have been able to help many trapped souls. But my powers as a ghost are limited. There is only so much I can do. But you two – you incredibly special children – can help me. You can act as my hands, and help some of the people trapped here as well. What do you say?"

Rachel bit her top lip in thought, but it was James who had a question. "What would we have to do to help?"

"You would need to meet some of the other ghosts here; listen to them, find out what they want and need, and do it for them if at all possible."

"Are any of the ones we'd help bad or scary?" Rachel asked.

"Scary is a relative term," James said grinning. "After all, they are all ghosts."

Rachel playfully punched him in the arm. "You know what I mean."

Tom calmly continued: "There are some 'bad' ghosts who could be helped. But I would not bring you to them. I understand you would be doing me an incredible favour. I would not risk your wellbeing around them. And, I am afraid, our time is short."

"Our time is short? What do you mean?" James asked.

"Tonight is a special night," Tom replied.

"In what way?" James frowned suspiciously.

"First you must prove yourselves. But if you do, then I have a most special and important task for you," he said with finality.

James and Rachel both sensed that the ghost wasn't going to tell them anything more for now. But both were intrigued about discovering more.

"So should we help?" James asked her.

"I think so," Rachel answered. "Those people deserve peace."

James nodded, but had one final, important question. "There's just one more thing I'd like to know, Tom. I'm sorry to say it – but why should we trust you?"

"Yeah," Rachel quickly said, backing him up. "Why were you at Port Arthur to begin with?"

They both saw him shuffle his feet nervously behind the podium. The ghost took a deep breath before he answered.

"I killed a man."

CHAPTER FOURTEEN

Rachel sat up in horror while James looked stunned. Thoughts of leaving quickly flashed through their minds.

"No," Tom said defensively, holding a hand up. "It wasn't what it sounds like. Please let me explain." Both of the kids fidgeted anxiously, unsure of whether they should run away or not. They hadn't bargained on hanging out with a killer ghost...

"Please let me tell my story." He paused, looking at them and their reactions. Finally, when neither of them moved, he began. "As you can tell from my accent, I am English. I was born and grew up in London. I came from an impoverished background – my parents both died when I was a young boy. But when I was twelve years old I managed to get a job as a servant for a wealthy judge who sat on the British High Court. I was one of six people working for him, living at his home, and over time I managed to work my way up. By twenty-five I became his head butler. I was so proud of myself back then. I had made it. I had broken my family's unlucky past. But I truly fear we were cursed for some reason."

Tom looked down on the podium. He looked like he was on the verge of tears. His voice was cracking. Though he was a confessed killer, James couldn't help but feel sorry for him. "What happened?" he asked.

"In 1837, as a twenty-eight-year-old, I still held the job, and was as proud as ever. But one day my employer was walking up the stairs to the front door of the house. Not knowing he was there, I opened the door out into him. He wasn't expecting the door to suddenly open, so he was completely unprepared.

"He was knocked backwards, and fell down the stairs. He hit his head on the cobbled road, and was killed instantly. I tried to save him, but there was nothing at all I could do."

"You were sent to Australia for that?" Rachel asked. "That's crazy. It was an accident."

Thomas Burke nodded. "It may have been an accident, but it was completely my fault and I never denied it. I was convicted for involuntary manslaughter, and I deserved to be punished. I took another man's life – the life of a man who had been good and kind to me."

The ghost closed his eyes for a moment, remembering the day.

"Sadly, as I told you, he was a judge, and he had many friends in the courts. So when I was sentenced they gave me twenty-one years transportation. You see, 'transportation' was the name given for sentencing overseas to Australia. To make matters worse, they had me sent to Port Arthur. Normally someone like me would never have gone here. It was a prison settlement for repeat offenders, but that was my first crime. The judges managed to pull a few favours, citing me as a special case, and I was sent here as extra punishment."

"Then what happened?" James asked anxiously.

"I was put on a ship called the *Augusta Jessie* and arrived in 1838. Port Arthur was only eight years old then – it was just exploding into life."

"We heard on the tour," Rachel agreed. "So many buildings here were constructed in 1835."

Tom nodded. "Well, I came here to serve twenty-one years. I took my punishment on the chin," he said massaging his square jaw, "and I served my time. It was extremely harsh, but I tried to make the best of it. I never spoke out of line, nor caused trouble – unlike many of the others. Port Arthur deserved its reputation for harsh treatment and tough criminals. Sadly I was caught in the middle. But in the end, I killed a man, had I not? I deserved it."

"No–" Rachel began.

"It is useless to argue," Tom insisted. "What is done is done. Nothing can change what happened. I then died here in 1871, sixty-two years old."

"Wait, that doesn't make sense," James said. "You said you were given twenty-one years – starting in 1838. That means you would have been freed in 1859. You would have been let out well before you died."

"And I was freed," Tom confirmed. "But by the living standards of that day, I was a fairly old man, and I had lived a very harsh life. My twenty-one years here were back-breaking and I could barely walk. I had no family to return to in England, and no money. They established the Paupers' Mess for people like me; to look after the old and crippled."

"You don't look old and crippled," Rachel said tenderly.

"No," Tom said with a weary smile. "I appear to you as I did when I was twenty-eight years old – at the time when my life was still perfect."

"But why are you still here?" she asked. "You realise you're dead – so why don't you move on?"

"To help others move on, as I told you. I took a man's life. I must redeem myself and cleanse my soul of the damage I have done."

"Don't you have anyone waiting for you on, umm ... the other side?" Rachel asked. "No wife? No kids?"

Tom shook his head sadly. "Now you know why it is so important that I have someone to help me save the others."

James and Rachel looked at each other for a moment, and then huddled together, whispering away in deep debate.

"Okay," James said finally, sitting up. "We'll help you."

Tom smiled, and if only for a moment his sad eyes regained some of their former life.

"Then let us go to our first ghost."

CHAPTER FIFTEEN

Tom led the kids down the small slope through the Government Gardens. Trees around them were rustling furiously: the wind was picking up even more than before.

The cold cut through James's thick jacket like a knife. He shivered, wondering where Tom was taking them. *Hopefully somewhere that isn't cold*, he mused. He already missed the warmth inside St David's Church.

Looking beside him, Rachel didn't look cold at all. If anything, she looked warm in her hot-pink jacket, and even appeared to be enjoying herself – taking light, almost skipping steps.

They walked together in darkness, the moon only occasionally peering through the clouds. Looking around the site, James could see their tour group coming towards them in the distance, from the direction of the Separate Prison. Looking at his watch, he realised that the tour would have ended, and they'd be returning back to the Visitor Centre.

"Rachel," he whispered and pointed to their right. "They're coming back. We should hide our bikes. Otherwise the others will know we're still here and they'll come looking for us." The last thing he wanted was Travis bumbling through the night looking for them... Although James did smile to himself thinking about Travis freezing his butt off even longer.

Telling Tom about their predicament, they snuck off around the Visitor Centre, stealthily retrieving their bikes and hiding them further away.

Just as they finished they saw Nick, Stacy and Travis emerging from the Centre.

"I wonder where Rachel and doofus went?" they overhead Travis saying.

The three kids looked around the building, searching for their missing friends' bikes. James, Rachel and Tom watched them from a safe distance, hidden in the bushes.

"I guess they had enough of you and left half way through the tour," Stacy said.

"How rude!" Travis said snobbishly.

"Well we aren't going to find them if they aren't here," Nick said, shrugging his shoulders.

"Okay, then let's go," Travis said.

An idea flashed in James' mind and he turned to Rachel and Tom with a devilish grin across his face. "Would you still like to play a prank on them?"

"Sure," Rachel said eagerly.

"We'll need your help for this one, Tom," he said quietly. The ghost nodded, glad to return a favour for his new friends. "Come up behind Travis – the skinnier boy wearing next to nothing, and blow into his ear or something. Do whatever you can to give him a good fright... Trust me, he deserves it."

Rachel had to suppress a laugh. It was a chance too good to pass up. "Please Tom?" she begged.

Tom winked back at them and then disappeared. A second later, he reappeared, directly behind Travis – who was leaning over his bike.

Tom leaned in and blew into the boy's ear.

"Quit it!" Travis yelled, spinning around and waving his arm.

Three metres away, Stacy and Nick looked at him questioningly. "Quit what?"

"Quit blowing into my ear."

"Err, we didn't," Nick defended.

"Sure. Right. Whatever," Travis said angrily, picking up his bike and hopping on.

Tom then reached out and put his hand over the back of Travis' neck. The boy felt his neck turn icy cold – but he also had the distinct sensation of being touched.

He spun around again, looking for the culprit. Nick and Stacy had mounted their bikes and were ready to set-off. No one else could have done it, but they were metres away.

Then he felt his cheek turn icy cold as well.

"Arggghh!" he screamed, slapping his cheek and trying to get the invisible hand off. He sped off on his bike and disappeared into the night at lightning pace, his screams echoing away into the distance.

Nick and Stacy looked at each other completely oblivious to what had just happened.

"Well," Nick said casually, "he finally snapped. We always knew it would happen one day. I guess we better go after him."

The pair sighed and slowly rode away, leaving James and Rachel covering their mouths and holding their stomachs to suppress their laughter.

Tom slowly walked over to them with a victorious look on his face. Momentarily forgetting he was a ghost, James swung his arm to slap Tom on the back, but his hand just passed straight through him.

"Oh no, I'm so sorry," he hastily apologised. "That didn't hurt or anything, did it?"

Tom waved him off. "Of course not."

Rachel couldn't stop grinning. "You're going to have to tell us what it's like to be a ghost. But brilliant work with Travis. That'll put him down a peg or two! The bully finally got what was coming to him."

"You're most welcome," Tom said. "And I would love to tell you about what it is like. But first we must get going."

The kids nodded. "Where are we going?"

"To the blacksmith. The bush is too thick to walk through at night. We will have to go back around."

"Where's the blacksmith?" James asked.

"Nowhere anymore," Tom replied cryptically, taking the lead as they set off again.

CHAPTER SIXTEEN

The trio were walking along the waterfront, in front of Canadian Cottage, with Rachel still giggling about Travis' breakneck exit.

"*Halt! Who goes there?*" a voice unexpectedly barked from somewhere in the darkness. "Announce yourselves or you will be fired upon!"

"It is I, Thomas Burke," their companion announced with a firm voice.

"Oh," the hidden voice said clumsily.

There was a sound of shuffling, and three men appeared from behind the small house. They all wore colonial-era red coats with bronze buttons and white leather belts strapped across their chests. Each wore a tall black hat with a regimental badge on the front, and two of them carried long-barrel rifles while the other had a pistol tucked into his trousers' belt.

There was no mistaking them for anything but nineteenth-century British soldiers.

"Hello there Tom," the tallest soldier said. He also had an English accent. "Didn't recognise you in the dark." The soldiers eyed James and Rachel suspiciously. "Are these two with you?"

Tom nodded in greeting.

"We've got ourselves some fleshies then," another soldier said.

"Fleshies?" James asked in confusion.

"You know – skin, meat, muscle," the tallest ghost replied. "A living person... Not like us."

"Oh, so you know you're dead as well?" Rachel asked.

"Of course we do," the soldier belted out.

"Then who are you?"

"Atten-shun!" The tallest soldier stepped forward. The other

68

two shuffled to stand side-by-side. "To your left, presenting Private Marks, and the gangly fellow beside him is Private Spencer."

"Who are you calling gangly, lanky?" Private Spencer accused the tallest ghost.

"Quiet in the ranks, or I'll have you court marshalled," the tallest ghost threatened.

"What are you going to do?" Spencer challenged. "Have me killed?"

All three ghosts roared with laughter. Even Tom chuckled – he'd seen their antics many times before.

The tallest ghost straightened up and introduced himself last. "And I, of course, am Captain Hunter."

"I'm James Masters," he said with a smile.

"Rachel Peters," she introduced, doing her best lady-like curtsey.

"A pleasure to be of service to you," Captain Hunter nodded.

"How goes tonight's patrol?" Tom asked.

"The usual rowdies are up and about. But nothing unusual to report ... apart from meeting those two," Captain Hunter replied, nodding towards the kids. "It's a rare treat to talk to some fleshies that can see us. It gets rather tiresome talking to the same crowd around here, doesn't it lads?" he asked his two subordinates.

"We find you boorish too, sir," Private Marks grinned. Beside him Private Spencer sniggered in agreement.

James looked the soldiers over, wondering what they were doing here if they – like Tom – knew they were dead. "So what's the story? Why are you still here if you are dead? Can you leave? Or are you stuck?"

"Oh we most certainly can leave, and we do. We each do tours of duty. Six months on, six months off," Captain Hunter explained. "When you sign up for the army, it's for life, and death. We're here to keep guard of the inmates that remain to this day. They were a nasty bunch in life – the worst in all of the mighty British Empire, and in death they can be little pests as well. A great number of you fleshies walk around here during the day.

Our job is to make sure they don't cause you too much trouble."

"Wow," James mumbled, "I didn't know all this stuff with ghosts was possible."

"You'll learn for yourself one day," Captain Hunter smiled. "But hopefully not for many years to come."

Before James and Rachel had a chance to ask more, Captain Hunter clicked the heels of his boots together and saluted the party before excusing himself and his men. The soldiers still had a patrol to conduct and marched off down the waterfront.

CHAPTER SEVENTEEN

Letting the soldiers do their work, the trio walked away from Canadian Cottage, passed the modern-day ferry terminal and headed down a dirt road to the blacksmith.

To their left they were flanked by a thicket of bushes and trees, while to their right the dark waters of Mason Cove sloshed against the shore. The road made a slight turn, and behind them the main buildings on the Port Arthur site fell away from sight. They couldn't see their destination yet either – the road kept curving.

They were fully exposed to the winds of the bay, and under his jacket James had to tuck his shirt into his jeans to try trapping body heat. For a moment he wondered how far away their destination was. They were out in the middle of nowhere now. A frightening thought gripped him: *Can we really trust Tom? What was all that talk about this being a "special day"?* For a moment James flicked on his flashlight and waved it around them. Directly ahead the road straightened and he saw their destination – or at least what he thought was their destination.

He could see the outline of a building that was actually the Shipwright's House behind a small field of grass. But as they walked closer he saw a man standing in the grass ahead of the house. Tom led them straight towards him.

As they approached the man, Tom began talking. "I have spent a long time trying to understand what this man talks about. I hope that with your help we can work it out. After all, three brains are better than one."

"What's his problem?" Rachel asked with concern.

"I'll let him tell you as best he can, and I'll try to fill in the gaps," Tom replied. "He used to be a convict here, but when he did his time they let him stay and get married because of how good he was at his work."

They stepped off the road and onto the grass directly next to the ink-black water.

Walking towards the man, James saw that he very much was a blacksmith, just as Tom had said. He wore a sooty long-sleeved shirt and brown trousers, but most importantly he had a large leather apron tied behind his back that went all the way to his feet – to protect from any fiery embers and metal.

"Rachel, James, meet Daegan Cleary. Say hello Daegan," Tom instructed.

"What canna' do for you?" Daegan said in a heavy Irish accent. "Has your horse bent a shoe? I canna' help I'm afraid. I'va lost me tools."

Tom turned to the kids. "Sadly Daegan is a trapped soul. He can't leave because he has unfinished business. As he said, he lost his tools, but he can't leave until he finds them. As a blacksmith, his tools were his life, so when he died and didn't have them, something was missing. So now do you see why I brought you here?"

James and Rachel both nodded.

"It gets worse though," Tom said. "When he speaks about his tools, he talks in riddles. I cannot decipher what he says."

Rachel blinked twice looking at the helpless ghost. He was pacing backwards and forwards along the grass. James shone his torch on the man and then the grass. He noticed that there was a metal strip running along the ground forming a rectangle that was about four metres long and three metres wide. There was a marking on the metal saying: "Blacksmith's Shop". This is where the blacksmith had been, and Daegan was pacing right in the middle of it.

"What happened to him?" James asked.

"He died in a fire that broke out in the shop," Tom said sadly.

"And he's been stuck here ever since?"

Tom nodded slowly.

"Well then," Rachel clapped her hands together. "We're just going to have to find those tools for him, aren't we?"

James walked up to stand right in front of the colonial blacksmith. "Excuse me Daegan?" The ghost looked up at him attentively. "What happened to your blacksmithing tools?"

"That infernal woman of nature with my heart took them!" the ghost seethed.

"Umm, I assume he's talking about his wife?" James asked Tom, who nodded in reply.

"Daegan, where did she take the tools?"

"They be at the bottom of what be preserved as much today as it were the day I died. Aye, they are, they are."

James looked at Rachel with a confused look on his face but continued his questioning. "Where is that?"

"I never understood," Daegan rambled on. "They be where she went to lose her mind. They always be there. I never understood why she went there, crazy woman."

Shrugging, James stepped back. "I've got nothing. I don't know what he's going on about."

Tom nodded. "That is pretty much all I can get out of him too. From other ghosts I did find out that his wife took the tools away and hid them from him on the day he died when they had an argument. He returned to his shop and was angry when the fire broke out. Ghosts often focus on the last thing they had on their mind before they died."

As if on cue, Daegan began mumbling again. "Pretty, so pretty. So pretty," he repeated.

"His hammer and stuff is pretty?" James asked rolling his eyes. "I think he has a screw loose."

James and Tom looked stumped but Rachel appeared to be onto something.

"Wait guys, I think I've got it!" She clapped her gloves together with happiness. "You actually worked it out James."

"Umm, what? What did I do?" James asked in confusion. "Tell us. We're all ears."

She paused for a moment, gathering her thoughts. "Okay, he talked about them being where it's as preserved today as it was in his time. Do I hear 'museum'?"

"Of course!" James exclaimed, but then frowned. "But it could be any museum."

"Nope," Rachel grinned. "You reminded me when you said he has a screw loose. He also said that his tools are where she went to lose her mind. Do you understand now?"

James shook his head. "Don't be a tease."

"Well, there's a museum here at Port Arthur. And guess what old building it's in? The Asylum – where they looked after the mentally ill. I did an assignment on it for school once."

Tom exhaled sharply and his face lit up. "Young lady, you are brilliant. The answer has been staring me in the face all along! I knew it was right to ask for your help."

"Think nothing of it," Rachel said modestly.

"So his blacksmith tools are on display in the museum, which is at the old Asylum?" James said, asking for clarification.

"Yep."

"Awesome," James exclaimed with a jump. "Then what are we waiting for?"

Rachel walked up to the old blacksmith and looked him in the eyes. "We'll bring you back your blacksmithing tools, Daegan. I promise."

The ghost looked glassy-eyed and almost swayed. "Pretty, so pretty," he said again.

"Watch out Rachel, I'd say the old charmer is talking about you," James joked.

"Oh stop it James," she said, her blushing cheeks flushing a bright pink that almost matched her jacket and gloves.

CHAPTER EIGHTEEN

Their feet crunched on the gravel as they walked along Tarleton Street towards the Asylum.

James reached into his pocket and again pulled out the brochure he'd picked up at Eaglehawk Neck. Flicking on his flashlight for a moment, he turned to a section on the Asylum, hoping to find out what to expect inside.

It was constructed in 1868, only eleven years before Port Arthur shut down as a prison. It was considered state of the art at the time, and held up to one hundred patients – not only from Port Arthur, but from across the entire region.

As they approached the building, James compared it to an old photo in the brochure. It was much smaller now – the bushfire in 1895 severely damaged it. In the past it had been an X-shape, but it had lost a 'wing'. Thankfully the beautiful old building had retained its imposing stone clock tower.

Tom led them up half a dozen stone stairs under the clock tower to the front door. The door unexpectedly popped and loudly creaked wide open.

"That's ... weird," James said hesitantly.

Without a second thought Rachel pushed him in. "There's a meeting hall and a restaurant to the side these days," she said as they entered the main room that housed the historical site's museum.

Ahead of them there were rows of tall displays with relics from all sorts of aspects of convict life. Rachel flicked her torch on as well, trying to find a light switch along the wall, but there weren't any to be seen in the large room. Disappointed, she returned to James and Tom.

"Okay, where do we start?" James asked. "Personally, I think we–"

"Shhh!" Rachel hushed him. She turned her head, listening. "I think I heard something moving."

She shone her torch to the other side of the room, but her view was blocked by the display cabinets.

"I think we should check it out," she said.

"Are you sure that's a good idea?" James asked in a low voice. "You remember what this place used to be, right?"

She nodded then shrugged. "So what?" she casually dismissed.

"Umm, my brochure said that they used to house violent patients here as well. You know – violent *crazy* people. That isn't the kind of ghost I want to meet."

She put her hands on her waist. "Oh c'mon. What can they do to us? If a ghost gives us any trouble I'll do a fly-kick straight through his head. That'll show him."

"Hey, I've seen *Ghostbusters*. They don't scare off that easily."

"Well, what do you want to do then?" she said crossly. "We need to find the tools for Daegan."

Tom watched the argument with amusement, but James finally gave in. "Okay. Fine."

"Good," Rachel said in triumph. "I'll lead the way if you're too scared."

Without waiting for him, she raised her flashlight, and began looking through the display aisles, searching for the source of the sound.

Half way down, a convict wearing a white coat and skullcap jumped out in front of her, poking his tongue out. He made a clichéd ghostly "ooOOOoooOOoo" noise and waved his arms around hysterically before he jumped for cover behind another row of displays.

Rachel turned around, mouthing "What the?" James could only shrug. Beside him Tom wore a blank expression that they couldn't read. Either he'd seen it all before, or he was worried.

Stepping forward carefully, Rachel was more curious about the ghost's behaviour than anything else.

She turned into the aisle the ghost had disappeared in, but he was standing there – waiting for her. He clapped his ghostly hands against a glass display case, causing it to lightly rattle.

Then he carefully walked towards her – making individual cat-like steps. Finally he reached out with his index finger and poked Rachel in the side.

She had enough of his antics.

"Umm, excuse me Mister Ghost, but *I can see you.*"

The ghost looked horrified and threw his hands to his face. "See ... me...? Eeeeeeeeee!"

He leapt up off the ground, shooting into the air and up *through* the ceiling. Rachel turned around, grinning. "See James? *Who you gonna call?*"

James groaned. "Who was that Tom?"

Their pale companion shrugged. "I have seen him before, but I've never found out who he is."

"Well, the loony bin is the right place for him," James said impatiently. "C'mon, let's go find those tools."

They decided to start their search back at the front of the room.

Looking over the displays, there were all sorts of relics from times past. There were shackles to put around convicts' legs and hands, axes they used to cut down trees, picks used for mining, and bowls and cups used to eat and drink from.

There were also displays of the clothes they and the soldiers used to wear – exactly like those worn by the ghosts James and Rachel had already encountered. Then there were guns carried by the soldiers, photos taken around Port Arthur, as well as books written by both the convicts and civilians.

On their first pass through the displays they didn't encounter anything that shouted *blacksmith* at them.

"What exactly are we looking for?" Rachel asked.

"To be honest, I'm not entirely sure what blacksmiths used," James admitted. "Hammers and stuff I guess. Tom?"

"Not my area either, I am afraid," the ghost said. "But I do know they used iron forks and hammers to hold and manipulate the metal on an anvil. They would have also needed a large pot to melt and heat metal in."

"Well I've seen a couple of hammers," James said hopefully. "No big forks, anvils, or pots though."

He led them to where he'd seen the hammers. One looked too flimsy to be used by a blacksmith, but the other looked thick and sturdy.

"If this is all there is, then we should take both just to be safe," James said.

Rachel turned to Tom, asking: "Did Daegan ever say what tools his wife took?"

"No. He never elaborates. He just talks about not being able to work because he lost his tools."

"Okay, then if this is all there is, we'll take both and bring them to him." James moved to open the lid of the display case that held both hammers.

"Wow, wait a second," Rachel scolded. "We can't just take them. That's stealing. It's bad enough that we're in here already after hours!"

James furrowed his brow for a moment as he thought, and then looked up with a grin. "Solved," he claimed.

Reaching into one of his pockets, he pulled out a mobile phone. "We can take a photo of the hammers," he explained.

"That should do it," Rachel agreed. "A much better suggestion."

Nodding, James navigated through the phone's menu and then lined up a couple of photos. The room was briefly illuminated with a couple of bright flashes.

After checking how the photos turned out, James returned the phone to his pocket. "I'm blaming you though if ghosts can't see mobile phone screens," he said with a glance at Rachel.

"I could see it," Tom said. "Modern technology never ceases to amaze me."

James remembered how Tom had said that he would follow visitors around. It must have been a remarkable experience for him to see everything progress over time. After all, James thought as he quickly did the sums in his head, Tom had been around for almost two-hundred years!

"We should make one more check to make sure we've covered everything," Tom said, interrupting James' thoughts. The kids agreed, but found nothing else in their second search.

Satisfied that they'd done all they could, they rushed back to Daegan at the site of the long-gone blacksmith's shop.

CHAPTER NINETEEN

Wendy Masters stood in the manager's office at the caravan park, frantically ringing the bell on the desk and yelling out to wake the manager.

"Hang on, hang on," a plump balding man said, rubbing the sleep away from his eyes as he staggered into the room. "What's going on?" he asked, his eyes still adjusting to the bright lights in his office.

"I need to use your phone," she said anxiously. "My son is missing and I need to call the police. My mobile isn't working for some reason so I can't call him."

The manager grunted, reaching under the desk to pull out a phone.

"I doubt it would, lady," he said, barely holding back a yawn. "We don't have much in the way of mobile phone reception out here." He then looked through a rolodex and found the number of the local police station.

"There you go. And if you'll excuse me, I'll be back in my nice warm bed. Good night," he said, stomping off and closing the door behind him.

James' mother rolled her eyes and quickly began dialling. It was answered on the sixth ring.

"Hello? My name is Wendy Masters. My son James is missing."

She went on to explain that they were on holidays and that he'd gone on a ghost tour, as well as saying he should have returned an hour ago.

"Yes I'm certain that something is wrong," she snarled into the phone. "This isn't like him!"

She listened impatiently to the police officer on the other end of the phone.

"Just look here! I'm going to keep on calling you until you say you'll go out there and look for him. You just do what you're paid to do."

Finally the officer on the other end gave in and agreed to go to look for him.

CHAPTER TWENTY

Constable Percy of the Carnarvon Police Station put his phone down carefully, and rubbed his ear.

"I just got the biggest serve from some out-of-towner with a missing kid out at Port Arthur, coming back late after a ghost tour. He's probably walking in through the door right now, but I promised his mum that I'd go take a look."

Putting his cup of tea down, Constable Percy stretched his arms and legs out while sitting back in his chair. Young but chubby, he perfectly fitted the doughnut-eating policeman stereotype. He rubbed his black moustache and yawned.

"Good," said Sergeant Cooper from the other side of the room. Tall and broad-chested, he was coming towards the end of his police career. He was re-writing one of Percy's poorly done reports, and was glad that his counterpart would leave him alone for a few minutes while he went to investigate. But then the phone rang again.

"Aww," Percy moaned. "That'll be the mum again. Can you take it, boss?"

Cooper sighed and reached over for the phone.

"Carnarvon Police Station, Sergeant Cooper speaking," he listened for a minute. "Your daughter you say Mrs Peters? ... At Port Arthur? ... I see." He rubbed his chin, deep in thought. "No, I'm sure it's nothing, but we'll go check it out just to be sure. Thank you, good night."

He sighed again. Rachel's mother had just rung as well to report her daughter missing, and two missing kids were too much responsibility to place at Constable Percy's bumbling feet. If Percy somehow found them, he was just the type to lose them again.

Fixing the report would have to wait for later.

"Okay Percy," Cooper grunted as he stood up. "Now we've got two missing kids at Port Arthur, so I'm coming along too. Let's ride."

Constable Percy's eyes flashed with excitement. "Oh goodie! Can I drive?"

CHAPTER TWENTY-ONE

They returned to the dockyard area with high hopes. Daegan's spirit seemed to sense that something was afoot as well. He stood facing them as they approached the site of his shop, and James thought that the ghost even cracked a hint of a smile.

James reached into his pocket. "Daegan, we've got a surprise for you..."

He pulled out his mobile phone in front of the expectant ghost and showed him the digital photos.

"My little darlings ... they be not my tools," the ghost said with an air of disappointment

James and Rachel stared at each other in disbelief.

"A-Are you certain?" James held the phone even closer, directly in front of the blacksmith's eyes.

"*They be not my tools!*" he howled into the night.

"But we were so sure," Rachel moaned. "It made perfect sense from the clues he gave."

"Daegan," Tom said gently. "Are your tools in the Asylum?"

"They be at the bottom of what be preserved as much today as it were the day I died," the ghost said just as he'd done before.

"So are they in the museum?" James asked in frustration.

"They be where she went to lose her mind. They always be there. I never understood why she went there, crazy woman."

"What tools did she take?" James continued questioning.

"Pretty, so pretty."

They looked at each other trying to make sense of what had just happened. Rachel's deduction from the ghost's clues had made perfect sense. But there weren't any other tools in the museum that could have possibly been used by a blacksmith.

"That infernal woman of nature with my heart took them!" he raged in anger. Suddenly he dropped his voice. "Pretty, so pretty. So pretty," he repeated. The ghost was stuck in a loop.

James threw his arms in the air. "So maybe we got it wrong? Maybe there's another place that matches what he's saying."

"*But where?*" Rachel pleaded.

"I don't know, but we'll work it out," James said confidently. He didn't feel as certain as he pretended, though. "He seems convinced that they still exist. So if he's right – and if they aren't being kept somewhere far away from Port Arthur – then we need to find a spot that would be good to hide some blacksmith's tools."

"What do you suggest?" Tom asked.

"Well, we can see most of the site from the Guard Tower. That would be a good start."

Rachel shrugged her shoulders in response. She couldn't think of anything better. Tom looked cagey – seemingly agreeing with the idea.

"Okay, then let's go again and find those tools."

"I think we should get our bikes," Rachel said. "We hid them along the way we need to go, and we've been running around all over the place. At least we can get around quicker on our bikes."

"Great idea."

James began walking away, but Rachel came up to Daegan again. "I promised that we'll get your tools back, and we won't let you down."

The ghost's gaze was far in the distance behind her. She felt terribly sorry for him, just wishing she could give him a hug and assure him that they would fulfil their promise. She turned around and began walking back to their bikes in the bush next to the Visitor Centre.

"Pretty, so pretty," they heard the ghost yet again – almost whispering – as they left.

"Next he'll be saying 'my precious' – *he* should be in the Asylum," James joked.

CHAPTER TWENTY-TWO

After retrieving their bikes, Tom said that he would meet them at the Guard Tower. He insisted that he didn't like the idea of having to float around at speed to keep up with the kids on their bikes. So James and Rachel would have to make the trip by themselves.

They rode carefully in the dark, not wanting to hit a pothole or branch and crash. Neither of them spoke, keeping their thoughts to themselves. It had been a crazy night. Seeing ghosts... Helping ghosts... It had all been so sudden. But strangely, neither of them was too scared. Okay, they were a little scared. But they realised that ghosts aren't fully creepy spooks. They are – or at least *were* – people just like them. Who knows – maybe they'd become ghosts someday too? And besides, what could ghosts do to them if they could see them coming?

As they rode they saw some shadows moving around. They were both certain that they were more ghosts. But they kept their distance from the shadows, concentrating on the task at hand.

As they rode past the Commandant's Office behind the huge Penitentiary, a harrowing scream tore into the night. Both of them skidded to a halt on the road.

James was wide-eyed, and gripped his handlebars tightly. The cry had been filled with so much pain, sadness and regret. It was the worst thing he'd ever heard in his life.

But Rachel just grinned back at him. "Too cool," she proclaimed. "You know what that was, right?"

James nodded slowly. "The boy in the tower."

"We're here to help, right?" she said fearlessly. "So let's investigate. It's right under where we're going anyway."

"We really should meet Tom first," James said nervously.

Another scream broke the night's silence. For a moment even

the crickets stopped their chirping.

"C'mon!" she waved her arm and sped off before he could protest.

"Oh man," James whimpered, his feet trembling on the pedals, "this is so stupid." He slowly rode the rest of the short distance after her.

Climbing off his bike, he saw that she was already waiting next to the thick door at the bottom of the Guard Tower. It was the door to the room that had been too wet for ammunition, so it had been used instead as a cell for condemned convicts that were waiting for their execution.

She put her ear to the door, wanting to hear whether there was any movement inside.

"I can't hear anything," she whispered to him. "Can you?"

James frowned, putting his ear to the door next to her.

"*Aarrrrrgghhhhiiieeee!!!*"

James leapt back from the door, his heart racing.

That settled it. The screaming was definitely coming from inside the condemned cell.

"On the count of three," Rachel whispered, grabbing the door's handle and holding her torch – turned off – in her hand.

"One..."

She braced herself, ready to rush in like it was a raid.

"Two..."

This is too much, James cried to himself.

"Three!"

She flung the door open as quickly as she could and flicked on her torch, illuminating the interior of the dank cell.

It was empty.

Oh thank you... James thought.

He carefully followed her inside, turning on his own flashlight and looking at the walls and ceiling.

"Maybe you scared him off with your Little Miss SWAT Team performance?"

"No, she didn't," an unannounced voice behind them suddenly said.

Both James and Rachel jumped forward in fright, spinning around and shining their torches at the doorway.

"Tom! We've already talked about you scaring the daylights out of me..." James clutched his chest. "I swear I can feel a heart attack coming on."

Rachel just laughed.

"No one ever sees the boy when he screams," Tom told them seriously. "I think it's just a residual memory in this room, rather than an actual ghost."

"What's a residual memory?" Rachel asked.

"A trapped moment in time," Tom explained. "A past event being replayed in the present, over and over again."

"That's so sad," she said, grimacing. "So we can't help him?"

Tom shook his head. "Sometimes he is also seen, but cannot be spoken to."

"But we can still help Daegan," James said, hoping to divert their attention and get away from the spooky room with the screaming ghost.

Tom and Rachel both agreed, and walked out of the cell.

James walked out last and closed the door behind them, hoping he'd never hear a hair-curling scream like that ever again.

CHAPTER TWENTY-THREE

They climbed up the stairs to the Guard Tower, walking through it and over to one of two small ramparts that was just big enough to fit the three of them.

Their eyes took a moment to adjust to the scene.

The Guard Tower and its two ramparts were positioned along a small hill. Soldiers on guard duty would have had a commanding view over the most important areas of the prison settlement.

The harbour was directly in front of them. The new ferry terminal was on the other side of the small cove, but the old stone jetty would have been directly under them. Slightly to their left were the huge ruins of the four-storey tall Penitentiary building, and next to it they could see the ruined Commandant's Office. If they stood on the same spot one hundred and fifty years earlier they would have seen dozens of more buildings.

"It's beautiful," Rachel commented, looking out to Mason Cove.

"It wasn't always like this," Tom reflected, shaking his head. "There was an astonishing number of buildings along this hill. It was dirty and packed with people. There were always ships waiting at anchor as well, to pack and unpack goods at the docks and warehouses. It is very different today. It is better," he added.

Looking further, James could see the church – still brightly lit by the spotlights, standing out like a beacon. He could also see St David's Church and the Parsonage where they'd been earlier. Behind them and to their left stood the ruined Hospital... He swore he could see someone moving along the top window. The problem was that there were no stairs to get up there...

"No," Tom said with finality, shaking his head. "You would not have liked it in my day. This was a bad place."

None of them spoke while they contemplated the scene. For

a moment the clouds cleared, and the moon illuminated Port Arthur to give them an even better view. Then, just as quickly, the site was gloomy again.

"So what are we looking for?" Rachel said, growing increasingly downcast.

"What did Daegan say again?" James asked.

Tom, who had heard the blacksmith repeat his riddles many times, recited: "That infernal woman of nature with my heart took them. They be at the bottom of what be preserved as much today as it were the day I died. They be where she went to lose her mind. They always be there. I never understood why she went there, crazy woman."

"And," James added, looking in Rachel's direction, "pretty, so pretty."

"There's no reason why the tools are here still," she said. "But assuming they are – they could be anywhere. This place is huge."

"No, they are here," James said firmly. "Daegan's wife hid them. She couldn't have hidden them far away. It's not like she drove a car to Hobart and hid them there," he poked his tongue out.

"Oh ha-ha, Mr Smarty Pants," Rachel retorted, mocking him. "Then where are they?"

"Can you please repeat what he said again, Tom?" The ghost then happily recited Daegan's words yet again.

Moonlight broke through as the clouds parted.

"Hang on," James exclaimed. "What's as preserved today as then?"

Both Tom and Rachel shrugged.

James didn't give up, looking to their left. "The gardens – the Government Gardens. Are they the same as they used to be?"

"Mostly," Tom said. "It hasn't greatly changed. The gardens were lost once, but they replanted them to be the same way."

"Well," James offered, "he said she was a 'woman of nature', and the gardens are preserved. Maybe we took 'where she went to lose her mind' too literally. Perhaps it means where she went to stop worrying and relax? Plus the gardens are pretty, right?

And Daegan didn't understand why she went there because he's a tough manly bloke who prefers molten steel, but maybe in his final moments he realised it after he had that argument with his wife."

Tom and Rachel both looked deep in thought, contemplating the idea.

"And," James continued, "look at the shape of the garden. It's like it has a top and bottom. Plus," he pointed up at the stars in the patchy sky, "the garden runs almost perfectly north. That means the 'bottom' of the garden is aligned to the south. South equals 'bottom', right?" He paused a moment, trying to gauge their reactions. "So what do you think? Could that be it?"

Rachel and Tom looked at each other and nodded. "Works for me."

For a moment they watched as a pair of torches swung around the Junior Medical Officer's House in the distance.

"Who is that?" James asked, puzzled.

"Don't know," Rachel said with a shrug.

"Well let's give them some space to be safe..." James replied anxiously. "Are we set?"

"Yep."

"Cool," James grinned broadly. "Then let's find some shovels and get digging!"

CHAPTER TWENTY-FOUR

After getting back on their bikes and trying to find a shovel – eventually fetching two from behind Canadian Cottage – the kids arrived at the bottom of the Government Gardens and were met there by Tom.

The garden was skirted by a dirt path, but the actual boundary was marked by an unpainted wooden fence and a number of trees.

"Okay, if my theory is correct, it'll be around here somewhere," James said.

They shone both of their torches around the inside of the fence. The ground there was flat and entirely covered by grass. There was no clear sign of where Daegan's wife would have buried the tools. Any earth she disturbed while digging would have long been covered over.

"It would have to be in a place where she'd remember it," James pondered. "She wouldn't have dug it in the middle of a field, in case she couldn't find the hole again."

"So close to the fence, maybe?" Rachel asked hopefully.

James stepped back and pursed his lips. "I wonder..." He got down on his knees and shone his torch around the corner of the garden. "There's a small bump in the ground over there. See it? It would make sense that the ground wouldn't settle properly if there was something under it."

He stood up and walked over, and taking a deep breath plunged his shovel into the earth. A few moments later Rachel joined him, and the pair dug together. Unable to pick anything up, Tom was left watching from the side.

"I feel like an archaeologist," Rachel exclaimed. "Searching for buried treasure..."

"You've got a very wild imagination," James teased. "Today

we're only searching for blacksmithing tools, I'm afraid."

Between shovelling dirt, Rachel shrugged. "I'll still be ecstatic when we find them, though. They've been buried for well over a hundred years, and no one else has found them. It might not make the front pages of the newspaper, but it'll be an important discovery to one person..."

A few minutes later, with the hole now around half a metre wide, and half a metre deep in the soft soil, James' shovel hit something that felt different.

"Stop!" he commanded just as Rachel was about to hack into the ground again. He turned his torch back on and looked into the hole. Sure enough, he could see some sort of brown, dirty fabric.

"We did it!" Rachel jumped up and down.

"Not just yet," James said cautiously. He tried to tug at the fabric, but a piece tore off. Years of being in the ground and getting soaked by water had turned it to mush. "We'll have to be careful. We don't want to damage the tools."

After more than a century the ground around the tools had compacted, so they couldn't use their hands easily to uncover it. Ever so slowly they used the tips of their shovels to delicately move dirt away.

Finally, a bag was completely uncovered.

"You can do the honours," James offered with a smile.

Rachel took off her fuzzy pink gloves and reached into the hole. The bag was in awful condition and it was literally coming apart in her hands. Uncovering its contents, she frowned.

"Daegan isn't going to be happy," she said.

The handful of tools inside were barely in better shape than the bag they were kept in. They were a yucky browny-orange colour from rust, and one piece – a chisel – was flaking bits of rusty metal, but it was probably the best preserved of the lot.

James sighed. He was as disappointed as Rachel was about the discovery. But since the tools hadn't been kept in a waterproof canvas bag, their poor condition was to be expected.

"I don't think we should move any of them except the chisel,"

James said. "The rest of them would probably disintegrate if we tried moving them."

Rachel nodded sadly. "And it would be best if we didn't tell him about the sorry state they're in either."

Dejected, they quickly filled-in the hole as best they could, and left a mound of dirt there. They agreed to tell site management about their discovery later.

Throwing the shovels aside, they hopped back on their bikes and returned to Daegan.

CHAPTER TWENTY-FIVE

With a great deal of trepidation, they approached the earth-bound blacksmith's ghost. Daegan looked like a small child, holding his hands and mumbling his same clues, over and over again.

The three slowly walked up to him. James gave the chisel back to Rachel, who stepped forward.

"Daegan...? Daegan," she caught his attention. "Look what we have for you..."

The ghost looked into her hands and broke into tears.

"My chisel, my beautiful chisel!"

He put his ghostly hands over it, coming as close to physically touching it as he could. He wept silently for a minute with his hands over Rachel's. None of them spoke, not sure of what to do or say.

Slowly, Daegan lifted his head. His expression was entirely different now. He no longer looked tortured and empty. "Thank ye, thank ye so much for saving me," he said joyfully. "It was like a spell. I was trapped, and unable to think of anything else. I canna' thank ye enough. I owe an eternity. Without ye I would be trapped here forever."

"It's okay Daegan," Rachel said grinning. "We're proud to have helped."

"Ye did more than help, lassie. Now I can move on." The ghost paused a moment. "I have to reward ye!"

"That's really not necessary," Rachel shook her head and knelt down to gently put the chisel onto the ground.

"Nay! The debt I owe canna' ever be repaid. But I can at least try."

The kids looked at him curiously, wondering what a ghost could possibly do to reward them.

"When I was alive I overheard a wee convict lad tell a story of theft. He said he was sent to Government Cottage to help carry the bags of a visiting dignitary. The visitor brought his young daughter with him, and at the first opportunity the convict stole a beautiful necklace from one of her bags. It was called the 'Necklace of Purity'. But as soon as they entered the house the young lass went to her bags, looking for her valuables."

Daegan became more and more animated as he continued the story. The inner strength of his soul was becoming stronger with every passing second after his century of entrapment – like a captive bird spreading its wings in freedom.

"She immediately told her Da' that the necklace was missing from her bag," the blacksmith continued. "The convict overheard all of this as he was carrying in the rest of their luggage. He also heard that they suspected that one of the convicts carrying their bags must'a been responsible. But before they could search him, he said that he hid the necklace behind the Sign of God in the house. Find the Sign, and you will find the necklace."

"The Necklace of Purity," Rachel repeated slowly, like she was in a trance. "It sounds beautiful."

"Aye," Daegan said. "The thieving lad said it be the most beautiful thing he ever did see. Sorry that I canna' offer ye more..."

"No, that's wonderful. Thank you Daegan." Her green eyes sparkled again in the moonlight.

"I'm afraid I don't know your names," the ghost said.

"Rachel," she said with a coy smile.

"I'm James."

Daegan just smiled at Tom – they had known each other in life. "Going to join me upstairs, Tommy?"

"Hopefully," Tom replied, sounding uncertain. "One day."

Daegan then nodded to each of them, giving them a final smile, and vanished by exploding into a dull light. A short breeze raced across their faces.

He was gone. But, amazingly, so was the chisel. The grass was bare.

CHAPTER TWENTY-SIX

They rested their bikes against the side of Government Cottage with its commanding view of the gardens where they'd found the tools. A flag mast stood in front of it, and the gardens ran almost to the front door.

Rachel was thrilled by the idea of finding the necklace as soon as possible, and had made James peddle hard to keep up with her. But when James saw the building he was less impressed.

Government Cottage was just a shell. Only brick walls remained. Everything else – the roof, glass windows, the entire interior – had disappeared years ago. He'd seen buildings like this at St Helena Island off Brisbane.

He doubted that they'd find anything at all within the ruined house. Rachel on the other hand looked even more excited with every passing moment, like she could sense the necklace coming closer.

They stepped inside. The ground was a mixture of moss, stone, and wooden boards laid-down for the tourists that visited the site. Their torches revealed that the bricks were a rich orange, but many of the walls inside the house were blackened. Evidently the house had burned down at some point, probably during the same bushfires that had damaged and destroyed so many other buildings on the site. It also seemed to be empty of ghosts; well, apart from Tom, who reappeared next to them when they arrived.

Walking around, nothing immediately stuck out to James. The rooms were completely bare of furniture. The ground they were walking on was the foundations. How could they find the necklace? If it had been here at all – and the convict hadn't lied about the theft – the necklace was probably found long ago by some lucky house guest or a servant.

"Whatever was in here is long gone," James complained, his voice echoing in the small rooms.

"Don't be so negative," Rachel scolded. She ran ahead of them, looking through the other rooms. Searching. Hunting.

"Women and their jewellery," Tom smirked with a low voice – careful that Rachel didn't hear him. James laughed.

While she zoomed around the house, James turned to the ghost. "So, you never told me what it's like."

"Like what is like?"

"Being a ghost. I mean, when I put my hand through you before, did it hurt?"

"No, I didn't even feel it," Tom replied. "The experience is different for all of us. Some have a full conscience – like me – who can think, remember our past lives, and are able to perceive what happens around us."

"This is going to sound insensitive; but do you have feelings?" James asked bashfully. "You might not physically feel pain – but do you still feel happiness and sadness? Do you miss your past life? Do you have hopes and dreams?"

"Dreams?" Tom sighed. "As far as aspirations go, yes. I have goals that I want to attain."

"Do you *actually* dream? Can you sleep?"

Tom shook his head. "That is truly the biggest curse of this 'state' that my soul is in. I never rest. The boredom can be heartbreaking. There are many other ghosts here, many of whom I do not wish to associate with; but talking to the same people over and over for over a hundred years gets repetitive. So to answer your earlier question, yes I do have feelings. I feel sadness... But happiness is something that I rarely have."

James felt so sorry for the ghost. "Can you travel? Can you move away from here?"

"No, I pledged to stay here to help, and because of that I am trapped here."

"So what do you do all of the time?" James asked. He couldn't imagine how caged-in he'd feel having an existence like that – forever tied to Port Arthur. It still was a prison.

"During the day I mostly follow visitors, listening to what they talk about, and trying to understand how the world has changed. During the night I try to help the others. I chose to stay here, but many others did not and they cannot bare it. I attempt to make them feel better as well."

James frowned. Being a ghost wasn't all it was cracked up to be. "Why are others trapped here?"

Tom paused for a moment, thinking about the other ghosts on the site before he continued. "Some are simply scared of death. They want to stay in this world. Others ... I am not sure. There are many bad, even evil people here, and I am not entirely sure what keeps them in this place. I like to think that their souls have some 'inner good' that keeps them here instead of infecting the rest of the world. Or perhaps the Reverend is right; maybe this is hell?"

James fiddled with his hands, trying to understand it all. He was getting a crash course in haunting, but he wasn't prepared for class.

The beam of light from Rachel's torch swung into their room, shining into his eyes.

"Come check this out," she said excitedly.

Has she found it? James thought in surprise.

She led him through the rooms of the ruined cottage and began counting. "One ... two ... three ... four..."

James didn't understand what she was talking about. He looked at her in bewilderment.

"The fireplaces, dummy," she said, shaking her head at him. "There are half a dozen of them in here."

"I guess they wanted to keep their valued guests warm and happy... Lord knows it's cold enough here in Tasmania."

Rachel pulled a face at him.

"So any luck finding it?" James asked.

"Not enough yet. But it's close. I just know it is."

James turned his torch back on and swung its beam around the room they were in – in the back-left of Government Cottage. It came to a rest on the fireplace. He tilted his head and blinked in surprise.

"No... It can't be!"

"What is it?" Rachel asked casually, not expecting him to have a nose for discovering fine jewellery.

"Where did Daegan say the necklace was again?"

"Umm," Rachel paused for a moment, trying to remember the blacksmith's exact words. "Under or behind the 'Sign of God' is what he said."

James stepped closer to the fireplace, and crouched down. "X marks the spot. Or rather, the Cross marks it."

Rachel shook her head. "I don't underst—" Then she saw what his torch was shining on.

A section of bricks were missing in the back of the fireplace. So instead of a flat wall there was an indentation in the back of the fireplace where the bricks were missing. The shape formed a crude cross.

"Oh my..." Rachel's eyes lit up, and she hugged James tightly from behind. "You are brilliant!"

James grinned sheepishly.

Rachel stepped back and rubbed her hands together excitedly. "So how are we going to do this?"

"Well, if this is the spot, then I assume there's a hollow behind one of the bricks. We'll need to be careful, though. This is a historic site. We can't damage it."

Rachel leaned forward into the old fireplace. Taking off a glove, she poked at the bricks at the back. Finally she found one that wobbled slightly.

"Just maybe, if I use my fingernails, I'll be able to pull it out..." she said, taking off her second glove.

Progress was agonising, but millimetre by millimetre the brick slid backwards. James leaned behind her, shining his torch over her shoulder and into the small cavity in the fireplace as it was revealed.

They both gasped. There is was, and it looked spectacular! The necklace was entirely made of shimmering gold and had a stunning green emerald pendant attached to it.

Seeing it, Rachel worked extra hard to get the rest of the brick out. "My fingers are sore," she protested, but fought on through the pain.

Finally the brick came out in her hand, and she collapsed backwards. Her legs, hands and back were all exhausted after leaning forwards for so long getting the brick out.

James reached in and retrieved the necklace. She stood up gingerly, looking anxiously at their prize.

"Here; it's for you," James said, reaching around her neck and securing the clasp. He stepped back to admire his handiwork. "It matches your eyes."

"Thank you." She leaned in and kissed him on the cheek.

Blushing, James turned away and stooped over to put the brick back into the fireplace as it had been.

Tom joined them and they all stood in silence a moment before he spoke. "Rachel, it looks lovely on you."

She did a little curtsey and beamed a gigantic smile.

"You have shown yourselves to be masters of solving problems," Tom said in approval. "I asked you to help with Daegan to prove your abilities to me, and you were worthy. You even solved his own puzzle to find the necklace. But there is another matter that I would like to ask you to help with, one of ... personal interest."

James and Rachel both nodded at the same time, without needing to ask for each other's opinion.

"Of course."

"We'd be honoured."

Tom smiled. "In that case, I will meet you at the Penitentiary – the main prison block."

Before either could ask him a question, he vanished.

CHAPTER TWENTY-SEVEN

Sergeant Cooper quickly walked down Tarleton Street. They'd searched high and low across the site for the missing kids and hadn't found anything.

Constable Percy was beside him, gnawing away hungrily at a chocolate bar. "You know boss," the young officer said between bites, "the kids probably left here after the tour and we've been looking in the wrong place. They're not here."

Stern-faced, Cooper nodded. "It's beginning to look that way."

Licking chocolate away from the corner of his mouth, Percy swung his torch around like he was in a disco. Cooper sighed. It was like babysitting a four-year-old at times. But then Percy's erratic torchlight caught something on the other side of the fence.

Cooper pointed his own flashlight towards the Government Gardens and his face lit-up. "Percy! I could kiss you."

"Steady on boss," his offsider said bashfully. "You weren't part of the deal when I married your daughter."

"Don't remind me," Sergeant Cooper rolled his eyes and approached the patch of dirt with a pair of shovels discarded on the side. The dirt was still a moist dark brown colour – freshly turned, no chance to dry yet.

"You wanted to kiss me over a pile of dirt?" Percy's face twisted. "This is an archaeological site, isn't it? The people here probably dig around the place all of the time. This doesn't have anything to do with the kids."

"Oh, doesn't it?" Cooper bent over and picked up a pink hair-band from the ground. "If you were a kid out here in the middle of the night – which you basically are, where would you go?"

"I'd get out of here," Percy replied without having to think. "This place is creepy as."

Cooper sighed. "They're close Perc. So close I can smell them."

CHAPTER TWENTY-EIGHT

James and Rachel walked with their bikes beside them in the dark, talking about the night so far. They went past the church and kept to the far side of the road beside the Parsonage. They then took a left-hand turn down Champ Street and strolled along the road towards Trentham house.

While James admired the wooden house's lush vegetable gardens, Rachel grabbed at his jacket.

He turned his head and saw a young woman, twenty years old at most, running towards them in the distance. She wore a Victorian-era long blue dress, a blue petticoat, a blue bonnet hat and carried a white lacy umbrella.

"The Lady in Blue," James whispered. He remembered back to Matthew their ghost tour guide saying that he was going to talk about her, but they hadn't heard any of it. "Is she meant to be good or bad?" he said nudging Rachel.

"I can't remember the story," she said fretfully.

He gulped. Tom had warned him that there were the ghosts of many people that he wouldn't even speak to. James swore that he once read about a woman who murdered someone at Port Arthur... Was she around? Without Tom, they were clueless.

As the woman came closer, James was struck by her beauty. She had the face of a movie star, and her long blonde hair flowed behind her.

"Stop staring," Rachel said, elbowing him in the side.

"Ouch," he rubbed his ribs. "I wasn't staring."

"Uh-huh." But Rachel also had to admit that the lady was beautiful, and the clothes she wore were simply stunning.

When the Lady in Blue was twenty-metres away she began waving her arms and calling out. "Please! Please talk to me! I need you to speak to me."

James and Rachel looked at each other thinking the same thing – *Does she belong in the Asylum too?*

"Please, I beg of you..." When neither of them replied at first, the beautiful lady reached out towards them and began crying.

It became too much for James. *The guide said that she's seen reaching out to people...* He stepped forward towards her. "Hey, hey – it's okay, we can talk to you."

The sobbing ghost looked up at him. A tear ran off her cheeks and fell to the ground where it disappeared. "Truly? You can see me? You can talk to me?"

"Of course we can," James replied. "What's the matter?"

"I've had the worst nightmare," she said in a soft upper-class English accent. "I can see ghosts. Ghastly spirits! Oh, it's most awful..."

James and Rachel both looked at her in confusion.

"No," she insisted, "it is true! They keep trying to speak to me, so I just run away from them, over and over again. It was the worst nightmare..." She began sobbing again. "Because I can talk to you, does that mean it's over now? Am I finally awake? That nightmare just wouldn't end."

"Oh, you poor dear," Rachel said to console her.

"That is not the worst of it," the Lady in Blue continued. "I would see real living people, but I couldn't speak to any of them. I'd come up to them, but they would act like they could not see me. I would wave my arms around, even jump up and down in a most undignified manner, but they wouldn't respond. Occasionally I think someone *can* see me, but when they do they look terrified, like I am some hideous monster. Do I really look that ugly?"

"No, never. You're beautiful," James replied. Rachel shot him a stare.

"Yes, you are beautiful," Rachel agreed, between clenched teeth.

"Then what is the problem? Why can I not wake up? I was running away from another ghost when I saw you walking down the road."

Sadness swept over James, realising that the lady didn't realise she was dead. "I think I know what's going on here," he said, looking at Rachel. She nodded to him in understanding. "What's your name?"

"Emily."

"Hey, that's my little sister's name too," he smiled.

"I am sure she's absolutely lovely," the ghost said, putting her hands together. "I love children; how old is she?"

"Two."

"Aww, such a beautiful age," Emily cooed.

Beautiful isn't the word for it, James thought bitterly.

"Well Emily, I'm James, and this is Rachel," he introduced. "We're here to help. So how about you tell us what the last thing you remember was before you fell asleep and the nightmare started?"

The ghost put a finger to her lips in thought. "I remember I was feeling dreadful."

"Why? What was the matter?"

"My stomach hurt so badly. I could barely move. The doctor was called, and he gave me something for the pain and to help me sleep. I'm afraid that is all I remember. After that the nightmare started."

"Why would your stomach hurt?" Rachel asked.

Emily smiled proudly. "I am with child." Suddenly her expression turned to grief. "Oh, no – the baby!"

When Rachel heard that she almost burst into tears. She looked at the beautiful woman, and though she hadn't noticed it before under the frilly dress, Emily had a bulge in her stomach. The poor woman had been pregnant when she died.

James saw Rachel's expression, and how she was struggling to control her emotions, so he had to help Emily himself.

"Emily, it's okay. You became a little sick, but the baby is okay. Rachel and I are going to help you see the baby, would you like that?"

The ghost fluttered her eyelids at him. "Really? You would do that for me?"

James smiled softly and nodded. Beside him, he heard Rachel sniffling.

But James knew it wasn't that easy. If she was trapped, then the only way he could help her pass over to "the other side" would be to tell her that she was dead. Worse still, he'd just learned from Tom that ghosts can still have real feelings – and Emily's tears before proved it. There was no easy way for him to do what he had to.

He leaned over to Rachel and whispered into her ear: "I need you to be strong now."

He stepped forward towards Emily, and began to feel tears swelling up in his own eyes, but blinking heavily he forced them back.

"Do you know what is wrong with me?" Emily asked.

James nodded. "Do you have a husband?"

"Yes," she smiled proudly. "He is a wonderful man – he run's the settlement's finances."

That's why she's seen around the Accountant's House, James thought, pursing his lips into a tight smile as well. "Would you like to see him as well?"

She nodded eagerly. "Oh William... I've missed him so much."

"I'm afraid I have bad news," he said gently.

"Oh no! Has something happened to William?" If it was possible for a ghost, she looked like she was about to faint.

"No, no. He's fine. In fact, he's waiting for you. I'm sorry to say the bad news is about *you*, Emily..."

"About me?"

James nodded sadly, and then closed his eyes a moment before taking in a deep breath. "Emily, the reason that you can see ghosts is because you passed on. You are a ghost yourself."

Emily looked bemused for a moment before her expression changed to anger. "How dare you! Getting my hopes up. Making me think my nightmare was over. You are an awful person!" She put heavy emphasis on *awful,* savaging James' feelings.

Rachel stepped in. "Emily, I'm afraid to say that he's right..."

"Balderdash!" she cried. "I expected better from you, a

member of the fairer gender." She reached into a pocket, pulling out a silk handkerchief and dabbing her eyes against it. "You are both cruel people. Good day to you."

She turned to leave, but Rachel called out to stop her.

"Wait! Please think about it. How long has this nightmare being going? Does it seem like years?"

Emily stood steadfast, refusing to acknowledge her.

"What about the clothes James and I are wearing? We're living over a hundred years after you died. People didn't wear what we have in your time."

Emily shook her head. Rachel reached into her pocket and pulled out her torch, turning it on.

Emily jumped back in fright as the light appeared. "You're a witch!"

"No, I'm not," Rachel shook her head. "Our technology has improved and we can do amazing things now."

"I'm not dead," Emily cried, putting her hands over her ears.

"Emily," James said loudly to get her attention again, "we aren't lying. Just think about it. Why can you see ghosts, and they can see you; but most living people can't see you or talk to you?"

"Because it's a nightmare," she said in denial.

"Pretend for a moment that it's not. It would make sense if you were dead."

"But I'm not dead. Look at me." She spun around, her dress twirling in the air. "I am here. I am real."

He didn't want to do this, but he couldn't think of any other way. "Emily, could you please put your hand out?"

She looked at him suspiciously, but hesitantly did so – her hand shaking in fear as she reached out.

James slowly put his hand over hers, and then dropped it – his hand passing through hers. Emily leapt back in sheer horror.

He stepped back to stand beside Rachel. "Do you see now?"

"I-I-I," she stammered, the unbelievable realisation creeping over her. She burst into tears and fell to the ground.

James reached out to hold Rachel's hand. There was only so much they could do for her. As much as they both wished that they could hug and properly comfort the distraught lady, they could only offer words, and now wasn't the time to speak.

She continued crying for what felt like an eternity, and in that time both James and Rachel felt tears run down their cheeks as they solemnly stood over her. For both of them it was the most heartbreaking thing either had ever experienced in their lives.

Finally, Emily got to her feet. The tears had stopped running, and she was almost unnervingly calm. A serene smile crossed her face. "I can see him. I can see my husband. He has a baby with him..."

"That's yours," Rachel whispered. "Go to them..."

Emily nodded, a peaceful smile crossing her face. Mouthing "thank you", she looked up into the sky and the beautiful vision faded from view.

CHAPTER TWENTY-NINE

Rachel fell into James' arms crying, mentally exhausted after their encounter with Emily's confused ghost.

"That poor, poor woman," she sobbed. "Imagine going through all that fear for so many years, and to find out that you were dead all along. And her poor baby..."

James patted her back softly. "We don't know what happened to the baby. Maybe they managed to deliver it. We don't know how far along she was. Maybe it was saved and lived a long, happy life and her husband took care of it."

James closed his eyes, and when he opened them Tom was standing in front of him. He slowly let go of Rachel and looked at the ghost.

"You did well, again," Tom said approvingly. "Once again you did something I never managed to do."

"You–you arranged this?" James stammered. "You knew that she would run into us."

Tom nodded slowly – guiltily. "Yes, I did. I made myself invisible and then saw which way you were going to the Penitentiary. Then I found Emily and appeared in front of her, making her run in your direction."

"That's awful!" Rachel protested as her face flushed red with anger.

"I swear it was the only way," the ghost said defensively. "She always ran away from us ghosts before we could speak to her and explain what happened. Even if we found a way to talk to her – you saw how frightened she was of ghosts. She wouldn't have believed us. I simply couldn't find a way to convince her that she was dead." He motioned to the kids. "But you – she trusted you. She knew you were alive, and I knew that you would be able to see her. Besides, I could not simply lead you to her. If she saw me with you she would have run away too. Sadly it was the only way. But good came of it. You managed to save her. Her unhappiness is over. Now she is with her husband – a good man who treated the convicts fairly – and her child. She has found the peace she deserves."

Rachel's expression softened after his explanation. "Well that settles it. I'm the *Ghost Whisperer!*" she proclaimed loudly and proudly."

"Ahh, so *that's* why we're stuck helping ghosts," James quipped in reply.

"So you forgive my actions?" Tom said cautiously.

They both nodded at the same time, but silently wished that he'd told them of the plan before.

"I am glad," the ghost said in relief. "But you have proven yourselves and your ability to help us ghosts yet again. I said when we first met that tonight is a special time. Now is the time that you find out why. Please, follow me."

Walking again with their bikes beside them, they set-off slowly to make the rest of the short distance to the biggest building at Port Arthur.

CHAPTER THIRTY

James stood in awe at the bottom of the Penitentiary. What remained of the building's four-storey frame was made out of scorched bricks. At night it was a hulking structure, and he hesitated to go inside.

Standing outside the front entrance, he could hear arguing and bickering among the prison's eternal inmates. The group of three stepped inside together and were met with a chorus of jeers and foul language – nineteenth-century style.

Turning on their flashlights, they illuminated just a small part of the large building. Shining the torch on the walls revealed evidence of fire damage. Between receiving rude remarks, James reached into his pocket and pulled out his brochure, interested to read about the building's history.

Built in the 1840s, it had originally been intended to be a flourmill and granary to store food, but due to its large size and Port Arthur's growth it was converted into a prison. On the ground level it had held one hundred and thirty-six of the foulest prisoners in small separate cells. These were the men shouting at them now. On the top level, four hundred and eighty better-behaved men were housed. In between were a dining hall, library and a chapel. Everything except the brick skeleton of the building was destroyed by bushfire twenty years after Port Arthur was closed.

Tom saw that James was reading about the building. "It made things better here," the ghost explained. "Before the Penitentiary was built there were up to two thousand convicts on the site. But this building changed the way prisoners were treated. There was a library with thirteen thousand books, and the dining hall was also used as a school room for the uneducated to learn."

"So it was the start of our modern prison system," James

realised, "trying to rehabilitate prisoners instead of just punishing them."

"It came too late for many though," Tom said sadly, shaking his head. "Those that came and left before it was built were not 'reformed'. Instead they faced harsh punishment and only became even more angry and violent towards authority, and were released back into society when their sentence was up."

"Even today our system is far from perfect," James told him.

They looked across and saw Rachel having an argument with one unruly inmate in a small cell – barely over a metre wide and just over two-metres long.

Waving his torch around, James saw that there were dozens of ghosts inside the cells. Amazingly, some even floated in the air – standing or sitting where their cells would have been on the levels above, except there wasn't a floor anymore.

"Come closer lassie!" one foul-looking convict said, his skin dirty and clothes torn. He snarled at her through rotten teeth and manic eyes. "Ol' John has a present for ya!"

"I want you to leave, and never come back," Rachel said defiantly to him.

The ghost looked shocked and, amazingly, disappeared in an instant.

Impressed, James walked up to her, asking: "Where did you get doozey from?"

"Miss Elizabeth Swann," she replied, leaning proudly against the empty cell.

"Who?"

"From *Pirates of the Caribbean*."

"Ohhh. So in that case, I guess I'm Captain Jack." James waved his torch around like a swashbuckling pirate.

Rachel giggled. "No, you're the pirate whose eye always falls out."

James glared at her and shook his head.

Suddenly the convict ghost reappeared behind her, yelling out "Boo!" before James could warn her.

Rachel screamed in shock and spun around.

It sounded like the entire Penitentiary was laughing at them. Their howls came from every corner of the building, echoing between the walls.

"You think you can just make us disappear like that?" the ghost accused. "You know nothing of what keeps us here! I wager you look down at us like scum. But I also wager you were born with a silver spoon in your mouth, missy. You know nothing of us."

"We'd better move on," Tom said, ushering them away from the cell – but further into the building.

The deeper they went the more concerned James began to feel. The profanities and jokes followed them as they walked – along with disconcerting whispers and sniggers.

"We are the damned!" one cried out.

Another made monkey noises.

Behind them, James swore he heard footsteps, but turning around he saw no one. *It's just our footsteps echoing, right?* he thought with a gulp.

He looked at Rachel, but if she was scared after her initial fright from the 'returning' convict she wasn't showing it.

They walked along a wooden board-way, constructed over the ground to protect the foundations from visitors walking over the stones. Tom kept leading them down the gantry, and then they encountered a staircase that spiralled upwards to what would have been the third level of the Penitentiary. It served as a viewing area for tourists, but James knew that Tom led them there for another reason.

Wordlessly, Tom began walking up the stairs. At the top was another wooden walkway. He went all the way to the end and then stopped.

Among a handful of ghosts slightly above them on what would have been the fourth level – the main dormitory where most of the convicts were kept – sat one ghost, suspended in mid-air. He looked to be in his thirties, but unbelievably haggard and worn. James could immediately tell that he hadn't had an easy life. The convict ghost's head was in his hands and he rocked backwards and forwards.

James could see that the ghost was repeating something; his lips slightly moving in the same motion: repeating one word over and over. But from his distance a few metres away, he couldn't make out what the word was.

"What's he saying?" Rachel asked, noticing the same thing.

"*Chastity*," Tom replied.

After what had happened with Emily – the Lady in Blue, James didn't think it was possible to feel even greater sadness. But he truly felt depressed looking at the poor shadow of a man sitting in front of them.

"You brought us here to help him," Rachel said – a statement more than a question.

"Yes I did," Tom nodded. He turned around, away from the other man. "His name is Edward, and he has a truly awful story. He was travelling with his wife to be free settlers in the colony in Hobart. But during the voyage he was wrongly accused of killing a man. Like me, he was given a sentence of twenty-one years." Tears welled up in Tom's eyes. "He was on the same ship as I was, the *Augusta Jessie*. I knew him well, and we were imprisoned together."

Tom cleared his throat to continue. "On the voyage he found out that his wife was pregnant with their first child. Soon after they arrived here the child was born. A daughter: *Chastity*. To be close to Edward, his wife took on a role as a maid at Eaglehawk Neck, and the guards allowed her and his daughter to visit occasionally. It kept his spirits up in an otherwise horrible place... But then, only four years after arriving, his wife died."

Tom pointed towards the man: "Edward was a convict, in a men's prison. There was no way they could allow him to keep a young girl in a place like this. Likewise, there was no way they could release a man convicted for manslaughter early, even if the evidence against him was nonexistent. Chastity was fostered off and quickly adopted. We never found out who she went to. I heard it was a wealthy family in Hobart Town, but nothing was ever confirmed. Sadly, Edward – having lost both his wife and daughter within the space of weeks – slowly went mad. He eventually volunteered to work in the coal mines to the north-west of here, and there he had a most unfortunate accident..."

James read between the lines and nodded his understanding. But a question remained: "So why is he here?"

"He searches for her," Tom revealed. "Today is special because it is the one day he is in Port Arthur. For the rest of the year he travels to and from England, six months each way, like the voyage that took him here. His is a tormented soul, desperate to find what he has lost."

"But why does he go searching the seas for his daughter?" Rachel asked in confusion.

"In life he lost his mind, I'm afraid. As ghosts we are often a reflection of who we were when we died. He found out that he was going to have a child while he was on the ship sailing here. He blamed himself for being the cause behind his wife becoming sick, and hence losing his daughter. Despite being innocent of committing any crime, his imprisonment led to the chain of events that led to this situation. He sees it all as his fault. But it is not."

"How do you know he was innocent?" James questioned.

"He told me so, and I would trust Edward with my life," Tom said with fierce conviction.

Rachel looked up at Edward's ghost again and sighed. "So what is the problem we need to solve?"

"You need to discover what happened to his daughter. Sadly, I am unable to move things in the physical world, and I can only travel within Port Arthur and talk to other spirits. So I am unable to discover what happened to Chastity. Somehow, I sense that she is close. I do not know how or why, but I sense her. Yet, I have not been able to find or contact her. That is why I am asking you to help me with this most important of tasks."

"Anything to help you Tom," James said enthusiastically.

"To the ends of the earth," Rachel declared with a huge grin.

"I am most glad, and I owe you a debt of gratitude that can never be repaid. But I am afraid there is a problem."

James frowned. "There's always a catch," he grumbled. "What

is it?"

"We have only until dawn to discover what happened to Chastity before her father departs on another lonely voyage." Tom pursed his lips and looked deflated – knowing the difficulty of the task ahead of them.

Looking at his watch James was flabbergasted. "That's only a few hours away!"

Tom began walking back where they came from, towards the stairs. His words hung in the air: "Then we had better get started."

CHAPTER THIRTY-ONE

Tom took them out of the Penitentiary and onto the thick, lush grass outside.

"What we need to search for first is the set of records that would have been made to find out what happened to Chasity. But everything has changed since the time they would have been used. They would have originally been kept in the Commandant's Office. But the building is only a shell now, so I am not entirely sure where to look."

"Well, if it would have been kept in the Commandant's Office, maybe the records are now kept in the Commandant's House?" Rachel suggested.

"That is my fear," Tom said carefully. "People are not welcomed in that house, and I am not allowed inside."

"Why not?" James asked with trepidation.

"The ghost of the Commandant still haunts the house. He is a very ... strict man."

James didn't like the sound of that.

"Well, if we're going to find out what happened to Edward's daughter then we're going to have to go in, aren't we James?" Rachel said, nudging him.

"Umm..."

"And you're going to join us, Tom," she added.

The ghost didn't look impressed either. "That would be most difficult if we were caught. The Commandant is a very—"

"–Strict man, yes, you told us," Rachel said impatiently. "But if you want to save your friend, then you have to come with us."

Tom nodded slowly.

"I guess we're *all* going then," James grudgingly conceded. "... Even me."

The Commandant's House was only a short distance away

from the Penitentiary, and right next to the Guard Tower that they'd already visited.

As they approached it, they could see how well preserved the house really was. Built in 1833, it started life as a four-room home, but rapidly expanded under the control of the various Commandants at Port Arthur, who each had different needs. In the end it became large enough to become a hotel when the prison shut down. Luckily it was saved from the bushfires, and it is one of the completely intact buildings on the site.

Walking up the uneven stairs, James was puzzled to see a climate-controlling door, to keep the temperature inside steady. He reached for the door, and heard a click. Frowning, he realised the door just unlocked itself.

"Curious," he murmured, as he opened the door and went inside. Immediately James understood why the fancy door was there: the house was fully furnished, exactly as it had been when Port Arthur was still an operational penal settlement. This way, when tourists walked in, the temperature would stay the same – helping to preserve what is inside.

James turned his flash light on for a moment, looking around at the rich furniture. He froze in surprise, seeing an older woman wearing a grey dress sitting in a rocking chair. She looked at him in disgust, like she hated the very thought of him being there.

Suddenly they heard voices outside: "James! Rachel!" the voices called out.

Immediately James fumbled around to turn off his flashlight. He looked back into the room, but saw that the woman was gone. However, the chair was left rocking by itself.

"Who are they?" Rachel urgently whispered, asking about the voices outside.

"I don't know," James replied.

They crept to the nearest window. They saw two torches moving through the gloom. The figures stopped at the junction between the Guard Tower, Commandant's Office, and the Penitentiary. They looked like they were debating something when one of them shone their torch on the other, illuminating his distinctive clothes.

"Oh no," Rachel moaned. "It's the fuzz."

"I beg your pardon?" Tom asked in confusion.

"The police."

"James!" one of them called out. "Rachel!" the second policeman followed.

"Are you in some kind of trouble with the authorities?" Tom asked in surprise.

"Our parents must be looking for us and called them," Rachel said apprehensively.

"Then you should go and turn yourselves in," the ghost suggested.

"Are you crazy?" Rachel asked. "If we go out there they'll take us home. Then we won't be able to help you find Chastity in time."

"That is most admirable of you," Tom said guardedly, "but will you not be in trouble if you don't return now?"

"Epic trouble. But we'll deal with that when we need to," Rachel said confidently. "Right James?"

"Sure," he said, offering a clenched smile. *But you don't know my mum...*

"Good," Rachel grinned as she peered over the windowsill and watched the policemen. "Then we'll wait for them to leave."

But instead of leaving, they saw one of the policemen order the other to look in their direction. Splitting up, the younger and larger of the two policemen began walking straight towards the Commandant's House.

James fretted while the policeman was preoccupied with looking at the ground and not tripping. Had the officer been more alert, he would have seen their bikes resting against the side of the house.

The policeman reached the bottom of the stairs, then lifted his hat and scratched his head with his torch before he began walking up.

"Tom, do something," Rachel hissed.

The ghost disappeared, and when the policeman was half

way up the stairs, his torch flickered and then went out. The confused man looked at the torch and then banged it with his hand without result. He shrugged and then walked up the rest of the stairs.

Instead of walking inside, he only looked through the front windows into the darkness inside. James and Rachel still had to hide underneath the windowsill, hoping the policeman wouldn't see them in the darkness.

"Oh no, I'm not going inside that spooky old house alone," they heard the officer say to himself through the glass window. "No one's stupid enough to go in there at night anyway."

Holding their breaths they heard his footsteps shuffling down the stone stairs, and disappear down the gravel pathway at the front of the house.

Tom suddenly reappeared, grinning.

"Nice one," Rachel enthused, getting up to her feet. "Now we can look through the house."

"Not so fast!" a voice cracked through the house.

"Oh no," Tom groaned.

They heard footsteps banging down the long hallway towards them. A man wearing a black uniform with impressive gold trimming on his shoulders appeared in the doorway. He strolled in like he owned the place.

"Just what do you think you are doing?" the man snapped.

"Commandant, sir, we do not mean to intrude," Tom said, straightening his back and standing tall.

"It is too late for that. What is the meaning of this?"

Rachel walked over and stood beside Tom. "We're searching for a missing girl, sir."

"Was I addressing you?" the Commandant scolded. "You will speak when spoken to. Have you no manners?"

Rachel lowered her head, put in her place.

"Commandant," Tom said apologetically in his most formal voice, "it is of upmost importance and haste that we examine the settlement's records to—"

"Nanny!" the Commandant yelled, cutting-off Tom in mid-sentence. His own manners were clearly lacking as well, James noted.

A blink of their eyes later the spooky old woman in grey reappeared – the same one James saw sitting in the rocking chair when they'd arrived.

"I sense trouble in these children," the Commandant told her. "Watch them carefully."

She nodded, and studied them with dark, beady eyes.

"Sir, I–" Tom tried to continue before being cut-off again.

"I have seen you around before," the Commandant observed. "What is your name?"

"Thomas Burke, sir."

"I will have the guards keep an extra special watch over you, and punishment arranged. It is strictly forbidden for convicts to enter my home!"

The Commandant clearly loved the sound of his own voice. He just couldn't stop yelling.

"Yes sir," Tom gulped nervously. "But I must speak to you about the purpose of our visit."

"I have no visitors after hours, Burke – convicts or otherwise. Good evening to you."

Tom hesitated and looked fearfully like he was going to leave, but James and Rachel stood firm.

The Commandant glared at them for their audacity to disregard his wishes. "I have come to accept that you ... people ... come during the day, but the night time is my time."

The look he shot them sent shivers down James' spine. In life the Commandant was a man used to having his way. He was not going to be happy if they didn't leave.

"With all due respect," Rachel boldly said, "we have to conduct a search. Good evening to you, sir. C'mon James."

James dropped his jaw, in part out of admiration of her courage, but mostly because she walked straight through the angry ghost. *We're in so much trouble now...* He raced after her.

Behind them, Tom and the Commandant erupted into an argument that shook the walls of the house.

He quickly caught up to her and reached out to stop her. She turned and jumped – pointing behind him.

James spun around, and stumbled backwards in shock.

The Nanny had silently been following him, only millimetres behind – literally like a shadow.

"I'm going to have a heart attack before the night is out," he moaned.

Regrouping herself, Rachel told him to suck it up, ignore her and get on with the search. They began looking through the fully furnished rooms, but didn't find anything.

Turning around as they walked, James saw that the Nanny didn't take steps to walk like the other ghosts they'd seen during the night. Instead she hovered over the ground, gliding like a "traditional" ghost. The sight was incredibly unnerving, and try as he could to put the thought aside, fear continued growing inside him.

Inside another room they thought they'd hit gold, finding an open handwritten book that looked like a ledger that had records. Instead, it only turned out to be a diary.

"You are most disrespectful children," Nanny suddenly said, scaring both of them as they walked into yet another room. "In my time, children respected their elders."

Neither of them replied.

"I see many children walking into this house during the day. I like to think about doing things to put them in their rightful place," she said wickedly.

"Like what?" Rachel said suspiciously.

The old nanny smiled deviously. "Only the things I used to do when I was still alive."

Out of nowhere a cane emerged, floating in the air towards them.

Suddenly James remembered something that the tour guide had told them. *They aren't just ghosts.* *"Some of the ghosts here are dangerous, and given the opportunity, they can hurt you."*

Rachel giggled. "See that James? She ain't no Mary Poppins!" she teased, putting on a Cockney accent.

The Nanny's eyes flashed with anger.

Without even moving her arms the door slammed shut behind her with a vicious *boom* that shook the walls. Then a huge cabinet slid effortlessly across the floor, blocking the door and their only exit.

The Nanny floated towards them, and stopped only centimetres away from both of their faces. "It's time for a lesson you will never forget."

Both James and Rachel were flung against the wall, pinned back by an incredible force, and unable to move. The evil woman tilted her head and they began sliding up towards the ceiling.

That was enough for both of them. In unison they screamed for help.

A moment later both Tom and the Commandant appeared in the centre of the room.

"*Drop them now!*" the Commandant bellowed. The Nanny's eyes widened and she disappeared, dropping the kids a metre to the ground with a loud thump.

Both James and Rachel's chests heaved a sigh of relief, but Rachel just picked herself up and stomped over to the Commandant.

"You have a poor choice of help, good sir!" she scolded him. "And we will not leave until you tell us where the records for the settlement are kept." Her face flashed red in anger. James just couldn't believe what he was seeing.

The Commandant looked at Tom, almost helplessly.

"I told you that they are determined," Tom said with a shrug.

"That you did," the Commandant shook his head. "It seems I was wrong, young lady. I have been informed of your quest by Mister Burke, and I am willing to offer my assistance, for the good of the settlement. As Commandant, I am tasked with maintaining the morale and wellbeing of the convicts that are sent to the colony. I have been told of a most unfortunate and personal circumstance that requires immediate attention."

The Commandant offered Rachel his gloved hand and nodded, by way of apology. "The settlement's records are not kept here, nor have they ever been. However, they can currently be found in the Accountant's House. I will ensure the door is unlocked for you. I also apologise for the actions of my house staff."

Rachel turned around to James – who was still sitting stunned on the floor – and flashed him a grin and a cheeky wink.

"But now you must leave," he commanded. "I wish you good luck." With that, he vanished.

"Come children," Tom directed with urgency, "before he … and she … return."

CHAPTER THIRTY-TWO

With little time to play with, they quickly slid the cabinet away from the door, and left the Commandant's House. But they had to be careful now, knowing that the police were looking for them. That meant not using the flashlights outside unless it was absolutely necessary.

Tom pointed to the distance at pair of dim lights moving around. "The policemen are at the Chaplain's House. We will have to be very watchful to avoid detection."

He led them along a long route – going past the waterfront, up through the Government Gardens, and then left to the Accountant's House where the Commandant said the records were kept. Thankfully they saw the policemen's lights moving away towards the Separate Prison and Asylum. They were safe for the moment.

They arrived back at the spot where James and Rachel had first separated from the tour group to play their prank on Travis and Nick. Only this time they walked into the house.

James understood now why the site records were kept here. The house had been converted into a learning centre. They moved around inside, looking for the records. They didn't have to search for long – there were all sorts of records in cabinets around the main room.

"Let's start with the birth registry," Rachel suggested.

"Fine by me," James confirmed.

"There is no need," Tom interrupted. "Chastity was born here at Port Arthur on February 19, 1839."

"Oh, well, in that case, let's see if we can work out where she went," Rachel said.

But James wasn't so sure, and got thinking. *Why does Tom know so much about Chastity? He keeps saying that this is an important personal matter... What if ... what if she's really his daughter?* However, James decided to keep his suspicions to himself for now.

They began sorting through the records and found a comprehensive marriage register, but that was no use to them. There was also an "Application for Marriage" register – convicts used to have to be given permission to marry.

"I tried to find out what happened to her, but they just wouldn't tell me because of how well I knew Edward. It was punishment," Tom said sadly.

"Would her adopted parents have changed her name?" Rachel asked.

"All I discovered was that a rich, childless couple from Hobart adopted her. She was a very pretty girl. She would have suited someone from the upper class. But she would have certainly adopted their surname, and it is quite likely that they also changed her Christian name to remove the stain of her father's convict past..."

James looked at Tom suspiciously as he told them what he had deduced. When he spoke of her "father's convict past" he looked like he personally hated saying the words.

"She could have had a long, happy life and her descendants are all over the place," Rachel said.

But the ghost looked pained. "No, I feel that she is close. I always have. Something happened to her, but I do not know what."

"Well, we have copies here of the original death registers for both Hobart and Port Arthur," Rachel said, holding up two books.

"Okay, how about you and Tom work together and look at the Hobart death register together because it's larger, and I'll look at Port Arthur," James suggested.

"Makes sense," Rachel said. Tom nodded his agreement.

They sat down at a separate desk behind James. He watched them for a moment. Rachel was sitting next to a ghost and looked completely at ease, like they were long-lost pals. He shook his head.

Sitting down as well, he began to look at the "Deaths in the settlement of Port Arthur" records.

Each handwritten entry had a number; a date of death and where they died; their name and birthplace; the person's gender; age; their "rank or profession"; and cause of death.

The dates of the deaths were relatively well spaced out – around one a week, so James was able to zoom through the records fairly quickly.

He became distracted by the "Births in the settlement of Port Arthur" register that was sitting close to him at his table. With Tom's back turned, James silently reached for it. *February 1839...*

He skimmed down to an entry on February 19. Name: "Chastity". Sex: "Female". Surname: "Burke". His eyes widened in shock. *She was his daughter! No wonder he didn't want us looking in the birth records.*

Before he could read the rest of the birth entry, James sensed movement behind him and quickly closed the book.

"Have you encountered any good fortune?" Tom asked him, turning around.

"Umm, no. No, I haven't," James said anxiously. "I'll keep looking."

He continued searching through the death register, with sweat forming on his brow. *What's Tom up to? Should I warn Rachel?*

He saw one cause of death that he had to comment on to break the tension. "Listen to this. 'Cause of death: 'By the visitation of God and in no other way.' Pretty cool, huh?"

Tom started to say something, but James ignored him. *What was it that the Reverend said back in the Parsonage?* James desperately tried to remember. *'There are no innocents here'? Was he actually trying to warn us about Tom?*

Gulping, James finished reading the Port Arthur death records and turned around. Rachel and Tom were having a hushed conversation about something.

"Found anything?" James asked.

Rachel turned in her seat to answer. "Maybe. We found a 'Mary Parkinson' that died in Hobart. Cause of death was listed as influenza – the flu. It has her age as 'five and a half'. She died on September 3, 1844. That would make her age almost perfectly the same as Chastity's. The birth records for Hobart are on our table as well, and we couldn't find her being born there."

"I'll check the Port Arthur one in that case," James said. "It's right here on my desk."

"No need," Tom said. "I can tell you there was no family named Parkinson here at the time."

More attempts to keep us from looking at the birth records from that time for Port Arthur! His heart rate began rising. "No, of course there wasn't," James said sarcastically.

"What's wrong with you?" Rachel asked disapprovingly at his tone.

"I'll tell you later..." he replied. *When Tom isn't around.*

"Well, let's look at the burial records and see what happened to Mary."

Since they already knew when Mary died, it was a simple case of looking up the date in the burial register. But they found nothing in the Hobart registry.

Then they looked at the similar Port Arthur registry...

Rachel read out the entry. "Name: Mary Parkinson. Abode: Hobart Town. When buried: September 10. Age: Five years." She looked up. "My God. They brought her from Hobart to Port Arthur. This is too much of a coincidence. It's got to be Chastity!"

"It appears that the authorities, or her adopted parents, decided that Mary was tied to this place for some reason," Tom replied carefully, not trying to get his hopes up prematurely. "It may not be her ... but you are right, Rachel, it is a large coincidence if it isn't her. We must act on it."

"Okay, so what do we do next?" James asked.

"Find her grave," Tom replied.

"And where would that be?"

Rachel read from the death register. "The Isle of the Dead."

"I beg your pardon?" James said nervously.

"The Isle is a little island in the bay. We can get out there easily. In French it's called Île des Morts," Rachel said wisely. "I learned that at school."

"I don't know what's creepier – the name, or that you listen at school," James teased.

"Oh har-har."

James threw his arms into the air in resignation. "Well that would just be perfect, wouldn't it? *The Isle of the Dead*. It's like something straight out of the plot for a book or a movie."

CHAPTER THIRTY-THREE

James had tried to get them to ride down to the docks, so Tom would leave them while they rode and he'd have a chance to talk to Rachel alone. But his plan was ruined when Tom convinced her that it would be best if they walked with their bikes and kept to the shadows in case the police spotted them.

James muttered angrily under his breath as they walked to Shipwright's House – right next to the Blacksmith's Shop where they had been earlier.

They arrived without incident, and they immediately saw a replica rowboat – a seaworthy copy of the design the convicts used to make at the dockyard – beside the house.

"It's perfect," Rachel said when they spotted it. "We'll row right over."

Looking out in the bay, around a kilometre out, they saw the dark outline of the Isle of the Dead. James shivered involuntarily just thinking about it.

Setting down their bikes, they walked over to the boat and dragged it down to the edge of the shore.

"You will have to leave me now," Tom said. "I cannot leave the mainland. I am tied to the settlement. I wish you luck finding Chastity. But before you go, I must tell you the truth."

"Ha, I knew it!" James cried out. "Chastity wasn't Edward's daughter. She was yours! I looked at the birth register when your back was turned. She was born Chastity Burke!"

Rachel looked shocked and deceived.

"No," Tom said firmly. "I *was* hiding my true relationship with Chastity from you. However, I am not her father... Edward is my brother."

Now it was James' turn to look shocked. *I saw the birth records,* his mind raced. But then he realised that he'd closed the book before reading who the father was.

"Tom, I'm so sorry," he begged in apology. "I just saw–"

Tom held up his hand. "It is my fault for not telling you the truth. Now I must tell you the whole story of what happened... Please, sit down."

Both of them sat down on the rocky shore.

Slowly, Tom began his explanation. "When I accidentally killed my employer, our parents were already dead. Edward and I were the only family we had, apart from his wife. We were so close – truly best friends. So when I was sentenced to transportation to Australia, he convinced his wife to follow me and start a new life here as free settlers. They were childless, and it was an adventure. Most of all, he and I would remain close to each other, and he would be able to visit me occasionally."

That awful pained look in his eyes that James saw when they first met had returned. The ghost spoke passionately and from the heart.

"One night on the voyage over here, he was seen getting into an argument with another man who had been drinking. The next morning the man was missing. The conclusion was that Edward had pushed him overboard. But he swore that he had not, and most likely the man fell overboard by himself and drowned. But it did not matter."

Tom sighed and lowered his voice. "As fate would have it, a new judge was travelling to Hobart on that same voyage. He had been a good friend of my deceased employer – the High Court judge. It appeared to him that Edward and I were two bad apples from the same tree. On the ship the new judge handed down his own sentence for Edward, which was confirmed in Hobart. It was only days after the man went missing that Edward found out that his wife was pregnant with their first and ultimately only child."

Tears began rolling down Thomas Burke's face. His was a tale of family tragedy all around. James remembered that Tom had told him that he came from a cursed family.

"You know the rest of the story," Tom whispered. "Chastity

was born. Four years later her mother died, and then she was taken away. Edward went insane from the loss, and I was alone – left to reflect on my sins for an eternity.

Tom straightened himself, as if James and Rachel were his judge and jury – evaluating his worth as a human being.

"It is also time that you learned the true reason why I remain here as a ghost. It was to save Edward from the insanity he held at the end of life and carried into death. I made a pledge to stay here as long as it takes to save him. Until the day Chastity and my brother are reunited, I am as trapped on Earth as he is."

Rachel looked dumbfounded at James. Everything had so much more riding on it now because of this. They had a real reason to evade the police now. They weren't just saving Edward – they were also saving their friend. This had become personal.

James glanced at his watch and saw that the time before dawn was running out. He lifted Rachel up from the ground by her waist and dragged her into the boat before she could protest.

"I swear we'll find her Tom," he promised with full conviction.

Leaning against the heavy wooden rowboat with newfound strength, he jumped in as he pushed off towards the Isle of the Dead.

CHAPTER THIRTY-FOUR

James took his turn to row towards the Isle first. The going was extremely tough. Out on the water the conditions were becoming increasingly difficult. The wind had picked-up even more, and waves lashed against the hull of their five-metre-long boat.

A boat like this would normally have two or three people rowing. But this one only came with one set of oars, so they could only row one at a time.

"I think," James hauled the oars towards him and sucked down air, "that there's a," he strained every muscle in his body with another row, "storm coming." Just then they heard thunder for the first time over the sound of sloshing water.

Rachel nodded silently. She knew his energy was quickly draining. Looking back she saw that they were about half way between the Isle of the Dead and Port Arthur penal settlement. It had taken a little over ten minutes to get this far, and James would probably only last a couple minutes more at most. She'd have to take over soon, if only for a few minutes to give him a breather.

Finally James' body gave-in and he slumped forward, his chest heaving in exhaustion.

With only one mount for the oars in the middle of the boat, James was unable to pass them to her, and they had to precariously change positions in the rolling boat.

Rachel sat down and eyed the oars with hatred and waited for James to take his position before she resumed rowing.

But she never got the chance.

A large wave struck the boat as he was steadying himself to sit down. James was rocked sideways and flung overboard. He desperately tried to catch the side of the boat but splashed down into the icy water.

Screaming, Rachel hung over the side – almost getting tossed out as well while the boat teetered on the edge of capsizing. She looked over the side and for a moment she couldn't see him, but then his head emerged for a moment.

"I can't swim!" James yelled to her before his head went under again.

He flailed his arms around in an uncoordinated attempt to stay afloat.

"Grab on!" Rachel called when he reappeared, stretching one of the oars towards him. He grasped it for dear life and Rachel reeled him in like a prized catch.

With his bulky clothes soaked with water he weighed nearly twice as much as normal, and already exhausted from the rowing, he just couldn't pull himself up on his own. Rachel had to dangle dangerously over the side, grabbing him by his legs, and helped to haul him back into the boat.

Rachel flashed her torch on for a moment to check him out and he was already turning blue. In the middle of winter the Tasmanian waters were close to freezing.

"Quickly! Take your clothes off," she ordered.

"But we barely know each other," James grinned while his teeth began chattering.

"Idiot. If you keep all those wet clothes on I guarantee that you'll freeze."

"But I'll freeze anyway if I take them off," he protested just as a light rain began to fall.

"Just do it!"

Grudgingly he stripped down to his underwear.

"Happy now?" Shaking, he hugged himself to stay warm.

"Not yet. Start rowing!" She pointed towards the vacant oars.

"You are nuts?" James yelled at her.

"You need to keep your core body temperature up," Rachel insisted, "or your body could go into shock. You don't need to row as hard as before, you already made your point Mr Tough Guy. But get going."

She was making some sense, not that James wanted to admit it. So he got to the oars and began rowing again – albeit with a sour look on his face.

But she was quickly proven right. While Rachel tried drying-out his clothes as best she could, he quickly began sweating again.

"Maybe this wasn't such a good idea," she said, thinking aloud and nervously tapping the side of the boat. "I'm a pretty experienced boater – my Dad takes me out here all the time. But these are some of the roughest waters in the world. At school they always warn us about it, and tell us not to go out here alone."

"I'm going to"–puff–"freeze when I get"–wheeze–"off this boat"–sniffle. He looked like a drowned rat.

"Don't worry, I've got a plan for that too," she assured him calmly. "But how come you can't swim? I thought you're from Brisbane."

"I am," he sulked.

"So what's the story? You should be a pro."

"No comment."

Rachel thought better of pushing it, and it took them another fifteen minutes, stroke by stroke, to reach their destination.

The current pushed them sideways, and although the jetty on the Isle of the Dead was only thirty-metres away, by the time they reached the small island James was physically finished and just wanted to get out of the boat. He aimed at the nearest bit of land – the rocky shore.

The wooden hull thumped and scraped against the rocks and Rachel jumped out, trying to pull it to higher ground – they didn't want to become stranded if the boat was pulled back into the water by the waves.

James got out of the boat and crumbled into a heap on the rocks, feeling like throwing up.

"There there," Rachel said, leaning over and patting his bare shoulders. "Auntie Rachel is here to make things better."

Looking up, he saw Rachel shove her fluffy pink jacket into his rubbery arms.

"Pink suits you," she grinned.

CHAPTER THIRTY-FIVE

Sergeant Cooper and Constable Percy trotted down the dirt road towards the old dockyard.

Cooper, older but far fitter, held his head up high as he jogged down the road, convinced that the kids must be there. They'd checked everywhere else since finding the clues in the Government Gardens. It was the last place left.

Trailing behind, his son-in-law and junior officer huffed and panted.

"Slow down, Dad," Percy called.

If anything, Cooper accelerated. "I've told you before not to call me dad!" It was bad enough knowing that Percy had married his daughter, let alone to be constantly reminded of it.

"Okay boss," Percy choked, wiping the light rain away from his face. At least Cooper had allowed them to return to their car to fetch their police-issue raincoats. "Are we there yet?"

Cooper didn't answer, and nearly sprinted the final hundred metres to the edge of the Port Arthur site.

He shone his powerful torch around to see the Shipwright's House and the Clerk of Works' House. Something metal reflected in the damp grass and he jogged towards it.

"Ahh, I've got you now," he exclaimed, studying the pair of glistening bikes. "You're around here somewhere. The nose knows!"

Percy jogged up beside him and promptly bent over, putting his hands against his knees. His heavy breathing sounded like a pregnant moose giving birth.

"What's the plan, Dad?"

"Dad?" Cooper raised his eyebrows. "Well, *son*, you're going to check those houses and make sure they aren't hiding in there. And make it snappy."

"Aww, I forgot the golden rule—" Percy sulked.

"Yes. Now move it."

While Percy made a laboured effort to search the two houses, Cooper surveyed the scene. *Why would they leave their bikes here?*

Percy strode back towards him. "Boss, I think I saw a light out on the Isle for a second."

Cooper snapped his head to look across the water. He couldn't see a light, but unless Percy was hallucinating it would explain why the kids left their bikes at the old dockyard. They'd left by boat.

"Hey, you don't suppose it could be ghosts?" Percy laughed.

Too serious for jokes, Cooper only grunted in response. "We need to get a boat."

"Where are we going to find one at this hour?" Percy asked.

"They keep a little tinny with an outboard motor at the ferry terminal for emergencies."

"A motor? Phew," Percy exhaled, "I wouldn't want to do the legwork and row out all the way out there. Especially in this weather."

"Ahh, but you *are* going to do the legwork. Run back and get the flashing police lights from the car. I'm not going out into the bay in the dark just so someone can run us over. *Especially* in this weather."

"Aww, but Da—boss," Percy quickly corrected, "we just came from the car."

"Atta boy. Then you already know the way and can run over there extra fast. I'll meet you at the jetty. Now go."

While Percy's large rear trotted away at half speed, Cooper turned back towards the Isle of the Dead.

"James Masters. Rachel Peters. Your time has come."

Ftizztzzz. He looked down as his torch suddenly blinked out.

CHAPTER THIRTY-SIX

James knew he had no other option but to accept the offered jacket. *Thank God Travis and Nick are gone*, he quietly praised. *Otherwise I'd never hear the end of it.* He put his arms through the jacket and zipped it all the way up, knowing full well that he looked ridiculous. It was a couple of sizes too small, but at least it was warm.

"Thank you," he said with as much pride as he could muster.

"You're most welcome," Rachel smirked. Under her jacket she'd still worn a light pullover. She was warm and dry for now, but the light rain would work its way through the fabric soon enough.

He put his legs back through his jeans before Rachel stopped him.

"You can't seriously be putting those back on," she scolded like a mother. "They're soaked."

"They'll dry out sooner if I wear them," James explained. "Besides, I'm not going to run around a place called the Isle of the Dead in a pink jacket and my underwear. I do have *some* dignity, you know."

She shrugged, conceding that he was going to be cold in either case.

He finished putting his jeans on and pinched his nose over the salty sea smell. Pulling out his soggy mobile phone he saw that it was deader than the Isle. Sighing, he reached for his t-shirt and own jacket. The flashlight was ruined as well, but he retrieved the information brochure and delicately opened it. Anything but the gentlest movements would tear the soggy paper.

"Can you please give me your flashlight?" James asked. There was a small shrub among the rocks, which he draped his shirt and jacket over, in a poor effort to dry them. "Alright, let's go find Chastity."

Walking off the rocky beach, they encountered their first ghost. Then another. And another. Shining the flashlight further, they saw that the Isle was literally crawling with ghosts. Hundreds of them.

"Just as I suspected," James said dejectedly.

He quickly looked at the brochure to see what they were up against.

The first burial on the Isle of the Dead occurred in 1831; a Private who died eight months after the settlement was first established. The Isle is only two acres in size, and roughly the shape of a kite – James and Rachel had landed right at the bottom of it. In places the Isle was covered in thick bush, but in others it was bare. A gentle slope went upwards from where they landed.

James read that the burials were separated by class. The bottom slope of the Isle was where the convicts were buried. The free people, both settlers and soldiers, were buried towards the top. James gave Rachel back her torch.

They began to carefully mill their way through the hordes of ghosts. Most looked like the ones they'd seen in the Penitentiary – filthy and skinny: worked to the bone. If this was how they'd looked in life it was no surprise that they'd died. From the looks of them, many had died young – a combination of hard labour, dreadful living conditions, and poor medicine.

When James told Rachel about the separate burial areas, they both wondered where they would find Chastity.

"She was free, but born to a convict," James said.

"And her adopted parents sent her back here for a reason," Rachel replied.

"Maybe they thought she should be buried with her father?"

"Or maybe so she could be with her mother?"

"Then we're back to square one," James said in disappointment. "She could be anywhere here."

Their task was compounded by the fact that there were next to no gravestones to be seen in the dark. Apart from a couple of special exceptions, convicts weren't allowed to have them.

"You know," James said with a grin as they stepped deeper onto the Isle, "there are officially one thousand one hundred people buried here, but some say the actual number is as high as two thousand. Do you know what that means?"

Rachel shook her head in doubt.

"Basically every step you're taking is over somebody's grave..."

"That's disgusting."

"Imagine all the worms and—"

"Ewww, stop it!" she shrieked. "I *hate* bugs."

James raised an eyebrow and sarcastically said: "Oh, so big brave Rachel Peters is afraid of a few creepy crawlies?"

Rachel was about to reply but suddenly a gang of eight ghosts appeared out of nowhere and began closing in on them from all around. One of them, a massive man with bulging muscles, even swung a ghostly log of wood attached to a chain over his head – with an abundance of wood at Port Arthur they never used the better known iron ball.

"That can't hurt us, can it?" James asked worryingly, looking at the makeshift weapon.

"I don't know," Rachel whispered. "But you saw what the Nanny was able to do..."

James nodded. "Let's make a run for it to the top of the Isle."

"Okay, on three," Rachel said tensely. "One ... tw—"

The gang pounced and leapt at them before she could finish. Both of them screamed and automatically ran as fast as they could.

Through the trees they could see a path and they aimed towards it. But James tripped over, and Rachel – with the working torch – ran off, leaving him in the dark.

"He's over here!" one of the ghosts called out.

Laughter closed in on him from the back and sides.

Something thick snapped. Not a twig, but a branch. James prayed that it was Rachel, and not the ghosts – whose powers they'd underestimated once already.

"James!" he heard Rachel calling out. He tried scrambling towards the sound of her voice but tripped over another fallen tree.

He began panicking. It was so dark; the clouds had completely obscured the moon. He'd fallen over twice and had become completely disorientated. Which way was he meant to go?

Suddenly he saw Rachel's light again, and she ran back towards him – carrying a branch.

"That was you that snapped the branch," James said in relief.

"No..." she replied slowly. "I just picked it up off the ground."

That meant someone else on the Isle was snap-happy... "Then we need to get out of here. *Fast.*"

She nodded and pulled him up in one swift motion, quickly leading him through the clump of trees towards the path. From there they were able to run – until the ghost with the swinging log jumped directly in front of them.

He swung, but both James and Rachel ducked under it and scampered up the slope.

"Over here," a voice called out to them. "Quickly! They're right behind you."

Not daring to look back, they blindly did as they were told. Suddenly a line of half a dozen soldiers appeared ahead, aiming their rifles at moving targets behind the kids' backs.

"Fire!" another soldier cried from behind the others while James and Rachel continued running.

The hill cracked with gunfire and a plume of smoke rose from the soldiers' guns.

They must have crossed some invisible threshold – a line between those that were "free" and "in bond", because suddenly the soldiers looked at ease, and, if anything, rather jovial.

James looked behind and saw that the convict gang had scattered.

"What the devil are you children doing here at night?" the leading soldier scolded. He was immaculately presented, and clearly showed pride in his appearance. "Don't you know how dangerous it is here?"

"We're ... we're here on a mission under the authority of the Commandant," James said. It was only a half lie; after all, the Commandant did know they were looking for Chastity.

That seemed to please the ghost. "I am Lieutenant Dawkins. I am in charge of this regiment." He pointed towards the half a dozen men in uniform. "If the Commandant has sent you, then I will offer you all possible assistance."

James puffed out his chest, trying to look as manly as possible in front of the troops. At least the Lieutenant hadn't made any comments about the pink jacket, but he heard some of the other soldier's giggling about something and he had his suspicions about the cause. "Thank you Lieutenant. We would be most grateful for any help you could afford us," he said formally.

Rachel spoke up. "But firstly, would you mind telling us what on earth is going on here?"

"I am afraid that the rabble–" he pointed towards the convicts "–is a nuisance that we in our current ... ahh, *form* ... are unable to take care of properly. Our weapons are useless against them, and they know it. But the men enjoy firing their firearms again. Thankfully this higher ground was specially blessed by the Reverend's ghost after he saw what the situation was, and they cannot enter our part anymore."

"So you *do* know that you're dead?" James asked.

The Lieutenant nodded. "I do; some others on the hill know as well. But many others do not – including some of my men."

James looked at Rachel and they were thinking the same thing: *We could try saving them, but there isn't time.*

They were there for Chastity.

CHAPTER THIRTY-SEVEN

After the excitement, the soldiers around them began to disperse and scatter around the top of the Isle.

James turned his attention back to Lieutenant Dawkins. "We're searching for a young girl called either Chastity Burke or Mary Parkinson. She was buried somewhere on the Isle. Do you know where?"

The Lieutenant paused for a moment and thought. "I am afraid I don't. But why would she have two names?"

"It's a long story and we're short on time," James sighed. "Then do you know if her ghost is around?"

"No, I do not."

James frowned in disappointment. "Well thank you Lieutenant. We may require your assistance later."

Dawkins nodded and turned around to join his men.

"So much for being a help," Rachel commented. "What are we going to do then?"

He looked around and noticed that the top of the Isle, where the free people were buried, had gravestones. "Let's check the gravestones first. It's a long shot, but maybe one of them is hers."

It took a couple of minutes, and a lot of the gravestones were badly worn and damaged – the local stone was very poor quality, so some of the names were obscured. But they were confident that she didn't appear on any of them.

"What now?" Rachel asked in frustration.

"Let's have a look around at the ghosts. Maybe she's one of them. After all, nearly two hundred free people were buried here."

Around thirty of their ghosts milled around on the top of the hill. There was a well-dressed family of five ghosts – including a young girl, but she was a year or two too old, and since she was with her family it obviously wasn't Chastity. They also walked to the boundary between the free and convicted, trying to spot a young girl among the convict ghosts. But on the lower half of the Isle they could only see men.

"We're stuffed," Rachel grumbled.

"It's not looking good," James admitted.

Rachel shone her torch along the ground and revealed a depression in the ground – what was left of a sunken grave. They both shuddered.

"Okay, well, we've come this far," he said as positively as he could. "Let's walk around one more time."

They both wandered off in different directions. James stuck to a boardwalk that had been constructed along the largest row of gravestones. He sighed to himself in the darkness and turned his head to the direction Rachel had gone. She'd walked along to the edge of the Isle, where there was thick vegetation before a two or three-metre-tall rock face.

He saw her outline, illuminated by her torch, but there was another light on her. Straining his eyes, there was something bright shining on her.

"Rachel!" he suddenly called out, running excitedly towards her across the boardwalk.

She turned around and walked over to him, but as she did so the bright spot faded and then disappeared.

"What did you do?" he exclaimed.

"Huh?" she asked in confusion.

"The necklace, Rach. It was glowing!"

"I didn't see it. Are you sure it wasn't just the reflection from my torch?" She was looking at him like he was crazy – exactly the same way as she'd done when he first saw Tom.

"Maybe..." He looked down in thought, but then raised his hand into the air. "Or maybe not. Go back over to that rock face. Don't look at me that way, get going!"

Rachel shook her head, but began walking back to the edge of the Isle.

After taking a dozen steps she looked down and gasped.

Thinking that she was imagining things, she turned off her torch.

The green emerald pendant on the necklace was glowing with a beautifully radiant light.

"Oh my God... James..."

"I see it."

"B-But why?" she stammered.

"This is a long shot," James said. "But what did the blacksmith say this necklace was called?"

"Umm, The Necklace of Purity, I think."

"Well, what if he got it wrong? Chastity means purity, right? Maybe it was 'Chastity's necklace' and Daegan misheard or just got the words mixed up, or the thieving convict tried to make it sound fancier while he was bragging to his mates about stealing it?"

"Sure makes sense," Rachel agreed. "But how could the necklace have been hers?"

"Well, Government Cottage was for important visitors, and Tom said she was adopted by a wealthy family in Hobart. What if her adopted dad was some kind of official – some government administrator or something – and he brought her with him to visit. And that's when the convict stole her necklace; but his theft was discovered before he could escape, so he hid it. And all of this could have happened before they changed her name to Mary, or maybe the name of the necklace was a reminder of her past."

"I'm liking it. But why is the necklace glowing now?"

"Because Chastity is close," James murmured.

"She can't be," Rachel exclaimed. "This is the edge of the Isle. It's just water out there."

"Give me the torch," James said, snatching it away from her grasp.

He turned it back on and began slowly surveying the rocks below them. After the 'cliff' there was a flat rocky table – about five metres wide – before the water began. It was solid rock, so no graves could have been dug there. But he continued to shine the torch along the edge of the Isle of the Dead.

Swinging it across, he finally saw something.

"There!" he cried out. "It's her. It must be."

A small girl wearing a long white dress was sitting on the edge of the rocks. Her legs hung over the side above the water and she was looking in the direction of Port Arthur.

"No wonder the other ghosts didn't know about her if she stays over there," Rachel whispered. "We've got to get down to her."

As James looked around for a safe way to get down to the girl, Rachel's scream tore into the night.

He snapped his head across just in time to see a terrifying sight.

A huge wave rose up, towering above the small girl on the ledge. For a moment time seemed to stop while the wave hung in the air, but nothing could stop it crashing down straight on top of her.

CHAPTER THIRTY-EIGHT

The wave smashed against the ledge and a giant plume of water flew high into the air.

Rachel put her hands to her mouth, certain that the small girl was washed out into the bay. James looked on, wide-eyed and holding his breath.

But as the water and spray fell back the girl reappeared, sitting exactly in the same spot, looking entirely dry and unruffled, and still staring out across the water towards Port Arthur.

"I thought we lost her..." Rachel gasped.

"It's easy to forget the whole 'ghost' thing, isn't it?" he replied with a trembling voice.

Looking around, they couldn't see a safe way to get down to her. The rocks were wet and slippery, and unlike the girl, they *could* be washed out if another big wave hit.

"We're going to have to call for her to come over," James sighed.

"*If* she can," Rachel said. "She might be locked into place or something..."

James shrugged and called out: "Chastity! Chastity, we're here to help you find your family!"

But his words had as much effect as the powerful wave. Nothing.

"Mary! Is that you Mary Parkinson?" Rachel tried instead.

Slowly, the girl turned her head towards Rachel's call.

"Mary! Can you come to us, please? We'd like to help you."

The small girl seemed uncertain at first, but she stood up carefully and walked towards them. Like a monkey she skilfully climbed the rocks up to where James and Rachel stood under a tree for some shelter from the drizzle.

She straightened herself in front of them. The young girl had pretty blue eyes, platted blonde hair and bare feet.

"That's a beautiful dress you have," Rachel said after she introduced James and herself to the girl, crouching down to her level.

"Thank you, miss," the girl ghost replied, playing with a white bow across her waist.

"Where did you get it?" Rachel enthused.

"Mummy got it for me. I like your necklace, too! I had one just like it ... but I lost it," she said sadly.

"Aww, sweetie, this one *is* yours," Rachel said with a tender smile. "We brought it with us to give to you."

"Truly?" she asked with a flutter of her eyes.

"Of course," Rachel answered.

"Could you please put it on for me?"

Rachel looked at James, her eyes pleading for help. How could a ghost wear a physical object?

"No harm in trying," he said with a shrug.

She nodded and took the necklace off, then reached over to attach it to Chastity's neck.

Amazingly the necklace didn't fall to the ground. It sat suspended in the air around the ghost's neck. The necklace's pendant pulsed brighter than ever with light.

"Well I'll be..." James said in shock. "We found our girl alright."

Rachel could only stare as the ghost spun around in delight.

"Thanking you most kindly, miss! I thought that I'd lost it forever."

"You very nearly did," Rachel said. "How come you're out here on the Isle?"

"I–I don't really know. Something has felt wrong. I feel ... empty."

"What's your name?" James asked.

"Mary Parkinson," she replied strongly.

James frowned. "Where do you live?"

"Hobart."

"Do you know what your daddy does?"

"He does something for the government. But I don't really

know what it is," the girl admitted.

James smiled to reassure her. "Does the name Chastity Burke mean anything to you?"

She squinted her eyes, thinking hard. "Sorry, sir, it doesn't."

"Please, call me James," he smiled. "Do you remember going to Port Arthur?"

"Oh yes! I love Port Arthur. Daddy used to take me often."

"Why were you looking out across the water to Port Arthur? Was it because the necklace was missing?"

The girl shook her head. "No. Something else, but I'm not sure what..."

Rachel stepped forward. "Mary, do you remember your other family?"

The little girl frowned and pouted. "What other family?"

Rachel didn't know if she was old enough to understand adoption, so she decided to keep it simple. "Before you had your mummy and daddy, you had another mummy and daddy. They loved you very much, but they both had to leave. So you got new parents. Do you remember that?"

She didn't look like she understood. "No," she said quietly.

James tried something else. *She probably doesn't really remember her Edward that well since she didn't get to visit him too much.* "Before your mummy and daddy took you to Port Arthur for trips, were you ever there before that?"

She tilted her head, as if something struck her. "Oh yes! I remember a nice lady taking me around. I liked her very much. I wonder what happened to her."

"Do you remember her taking you anywhere in particular? Did you ever go to see some other people there?"

"Of course! We used to go to the prison. I didn't like it there. It was *very* smelly," she said, pulling a face and wrinkling her nose. "But there were a couple of very nice men there."

"Were their names Edward and Thomas?" he asked.

"Oh ... yes! Edward used to call me his Little Possum," she giggled. "He used to say I was the best daughter in the world. Why would he say that? 'Chastity,' he'd say, 'I love you and your mother to the ends of the earth.'"

"Edward is your father..." James slowly said.

But she wasn't listening. "We had the best day ever once! One time he wasn't in the prison. They let him out and he had to walk around with a shuffle because he had these silly irons around his legs! But we went to the water and he and Mummy—"

Rachel gasped – she was remembering her past.

"Don't say anything," James whispered over to her. "She's working it out herself..."

"—were splashing each other," the ghost giggled again thinking back at the memory. "I laughed so hard. But then Mummy became sick soon after, and I never saw either of them again. I wish I could see them again... I remember now!"

"We can take you to see Edward – your dad," Rachel smiled. "And Thomas as well – your uncle."

The ghost's jaw dropped. "My Daddy?"

"Yep! It's complicated. Adult stuff. But he'd like to see you very, very much. He misses you with all his heart. We can take you to see him."

"Really? Truly?"

"We'd love to take you," Rachel said gently.

"So do you remember now?" James asked. "Do you know who Chastity Burke is?"

She narrowed her eyes at him. "Of course. I am."

Both James and Rachel sighed in relief. Chastity didn't seem to understand what the fuss was about.

But then the ghost frowned and looked at James in the pink jacket. "Say, you look awfully funny."

Rachel burst out laughing. "I know; he can be very silly."

"Great, now there are two girls laughing at me," he rolled his eyes and turned away towards the bay. All of a sudden his eyes widened. "Oh no... Rach... We're in big trouble!"

She turned around as well and saw a flashing red and blue light speeding towards them in the cove.

CHAPTER THIRTY-NINE

"It's the police," Rachel cried out.

"We need to get out of here," James urged. "*Now!*"

"Chastity, sweetie," Rachel said as calmly as she could manage. "We need to go to the boat now. We're going on a bit of an adventure to get you to your daddy."

"Yay! An adventure!" their little companion squealed and clapped her small hands together, unaware that they were in a race against time in more ways than one.

She held out her hand for Rachel to hold. Rachel had little option but to hold her hand out as well. But incredibly she could feel a tingling sensation on her skin as Chastity's ghostly hand touched hers.

James led them back to the main cemetery area, where the majority of the headstones were. But the scene was completely different to the one they'd left only minutes ago.

Dozens of angry convicts stood along the boundary between the free and imprisoned part of the Isle. Many of the spirits of the free people were cowering and looking terrified.

"We want the intruders!" one of the nastiest-looking convicts snarled at the small number of soldiers.

James quickly found Lieutenant Dawkins. "We need to get off the Isle now," James yelled at him over the noise of the other ghosts.

"The convicts are awfully restless," the soldier replied uneasily. "We could have a full rebellion on our hands if we aren't careful. This needs to be resolved tactfully."

"Need I remind you that we are here under the specific instructions of the Commandant? Get us off this island," James barked at him like he was the Lieutenant's superior officer. "Our boat is on the lower shore."

"Very well," the soldier cleared his throat. "They are unable to enter our holy area, but we can enter theirs. We can create a distraction for you to sneak around the side."

"There's no time for sneaking," James fumed. "We have to leave *now*. Right down the middle. It's the quickest way."

"I see," the Lieutenant sighed and closed his eyes for a moment. "Men, prepare for a frontal assault!"

His regiment of six soldiers quickly attached bayonets to their rifles and grinned at each other, raring for action.

"When you are ready," the Lieutenant told James.

James turned to Rachel and Chastity. "The boat is less than a hundred metres away. Stick to the path all the way to the end. Don't stop running no matter what."

Rachel nodded grimly. Chastity couldn't wipe the smile off her face. "Just take my hand and don't stop, okay sweetie?" The ghost eagerly nodded.

"We're ready," James told the solider. "Cover us as best you can."

The Lieutenant saluted and turned to the line of soldiers. "Ready. Aim. Fire!"

Their guns blasted and sent some of the convicts scurrying away and forming a hole for the kids to escape through.

"Charge!" the Lieutenant yelled – and the soldiers raced after the kids.

James took the lead with the flashlight, with Rachel and Chastity following.

Some of the convict ghosts didn't appear to be taking part in the fight, but many were.

They jumped at the kids from all sides.

One convict swung a ghostly hammer at James and hit him on the shoulder. The impact hurt him enough to reel sideways, but thankfully it didn't feel as hard as a real hammer.

They kept running, with shouting all around them. The soldiers acting as diversions were working, and many of the ghosts charged at them instead of the kids.

But just as they were coming to the bottom of the Isle, a

short, stumpy ghost appeared. In his hands he held a freshly broken branch – a real branch. The type that really hurt.

James stopped – the ghost had eyes only for him. "Get her to the boat," he yelled to Rachel. "I'll meet you there."

The two girls raced past, leaving James alone with the dangerous ghost, and completely unarmed.

James danced left, then right, trying to fake the ghost, but the ghost anticipated every move with a throaty cackle.

Finally the ghost sprung and leapt at James, the branch up in the air and hurtling towards his head.

But instead of going right or left, James went straight ahead and *through* the ghost, who hadn't been expecting that at all. He heard the branch *swoosh* narrowly past him. But before the ghost could turn back around and chase after him, James was gone and scrambling over the rocky shore towards the boat.

He hit the boat at top speed and pushed it off the rocks with all his might, launching it straight into the water. His shoes and the bottom of his jeans got wet again, but he dived into the boat, and to safety.

"Oh no; my jacket and t-shirt," he moaned, looking back to shore.

"Don't worry," Rachel said – having taken position at the oars and rowing as fast as she could away from the Isle. "I got them for you. They're actually pretty dry now. The wind must have done it."

Just as she said that, the sky opened up and it began pouring rain.

CHAPTER FORTY

Looking behind through the driving rain, James could see the police boat just metres away from the Isle of the Dead jetty. If the police looked in their direction they'd surely be seen, but thankfully they were preoccupied with navigating to the jetty.

"Where do we go?" Rachel hissed. She'd realised how hard it is to row a heavy boat on your own.

"There!" James pointed at land less than a hundred metres away – on the opposite side of the bay from Port Arthur. "But row a little bit further away, so they can't see where we land. We should also look for some shelter."

The wind had really picked up now, and the waves were dangerously big. They were definitely in a storm. If it took them another twenty or thirty minutes to get to Port Arthur there was a very real chance that they'd be swamped or capsize and roll over.

Rachel nodded in the direction of the nearest land, saying, "That's where Point Puer boys' prison was," and continued rowing with clenched teeth. She aimed at a small sandy beach a couple of hundred metres down the shore.

They landed on the beach almost like surf lifesavers in their boats – using the waves to pick up speed. The boat came to a gentle rest against the sand, and James and Rachel both jumped out and pulled it onto higher ground.

Looking around to assess their surroundings, James spotted a dim light through the trees. "Is that a house or something up there?" he asked.

"I really don't know," she admitted. "I've never actually been out here... They say there're a lot of snakes..."

"The creepy crawly thing again?"

Rachel nodded, and James wasn't going to argue. Though he

knew that Tasmania didn't have as many poisonous snakes as mainland Australia, they still existed. He bent over, tucking his jeans into his socks – to give any snakes as little thinly covered skin to aim at as possible around their ankles. Seeing what he was doing, Rachel copied.

"So what's the plan now?" she asked.

He looked at his watch. They still had a little time. "We may as well wait a little while and check out that light. We can't go back out there with the conditions like they are now. It'll give the cops a little bit of time to clear off, and maybe we can dry out a little as well if the rain stops or we find somewhere to hide."

Rachel agreed, and they walked up a steep incline with Chastity – who refused to walk anywhere without holding Rachel's hand.

At the top they were met by a man with a trimmed beard dressed in a blue coat, black leather cap, and carrying a lantern just like the ones on the ghost tour. He'd been the source of the light. Except, this man was a ghost.

"What in the blazers are you doing out here in weather like this?" the man gawked at them. "I suppose you aren't locals if you do not know you should be inside while *this* is going on." He waved his free arm around, gesturing at the rain. Before any of them could get a word in, he asked: "I like to know what I am getting into. So where are you from?"

"Err, I'm from Brisbane," James said.

"Ahh, I was correct then. A new arrival. Still no excuse to be out here. No excuse at all," he exclaimed with a dry laugh that only slightly putting the kids at ease. "I am the Superintendant of Point Puer, and you will henceforth address me as sir. And you ... young ladies... Fraternising with the opposite gender just will not do! This is a boys' prison. Heavens know why they sent you two here, but I cannot have you sent back to Port Arthur in this atrocious weather. It would be just like them to send their troubles here when I can't send you back. Quickly, follow me."

"Yes ... sir," they mumbled, shooting each other confused glances as they walked after him.

"What are you doing here?" the Superintendant asked.

"Looking for shelter, sir."

He eyed them over. "So then, you are not completely without sense. But I can see your waterlogged state, and that was not the intention of my question. A boy of your age should know better than that!"

What on earth is this guy on about? James wondered.

"We will have to work on you," the ghost mused. "The point of my question was to ask why you have been sent here to my station."

"Umm, sent? I'm here on holidays, sir," James replied.

The Superintendant's face turned a bright red. "Holidays! You call this holidaying? The nerve of you!"

"I didn't mean it that way, sir," James said defensively. "We were chased here by the police–"

"The police?" he boomed. "That would be right. They send the worst to me, when they should be kept in the penitentiary with the adults!" He muttered to himself.

"We really didn't mean to intrude," Rachel said as politely as she could.

"Oh no, this is just my job," the Superintendant shook his head. "A posting on the far side of the world to look after you lot. No, you are not intruding at all. Not on a beautiful night like this! Well, I have just the place for you, and you will get all the shelter you need. And I will give you all the time you need to dry-off." He chuckled again.

He led them on for a short while in silence. The bush had really taken over at Point Puer. There were stony remains of buildings all around them, but they couldn't see any ones left standing, and nothing that would provide shelter.

Glancing to his side, James saw Rachel still holding Chastity's hand, but now the young girl was skipping along merrily.

After walking for another minute the Superintendant stopped. "Right, here we are. Down there – follow me."

He stood beside a rocky outcrop on the ground, and then stepped down and began walking down into the ground before disappearing.

"There must be a stairway blocked by the rocks," James deduced.

"We don't have time for this," Rachel dismissed.

Just then a lightning bolt struck a tree only a hundred metres away, and brought with it even more rain. The thunderclap was so unexpected, and so loud that it shook their eardrums. It took them only a stunned moment to jolt into action.

"Get down! Lightning is attracted to tall objects – including people," James shouted. "We can't hide under trees now either," he said, quickly getting onto his knees and beginning to throw rocks aside to clear the blocked stairway.

Rachel got down and joined him, and together they made rapid progress, clearing a hole big enough to wriggle through in only a couple of nerve-wracking minutes while thunder and lightning cracked around them.

Brushing themselves off, Rachel turned on her torch and saw they were standing in a small room dug underground. Green moss covered the walls and roof, but it was relatively dry.

The Superintendant was standing in the middle of the small room and then walked towards them.

"Right, for making me wait so long I will double your time here! Expect a flogging at first light in the morning."

Baffled, James frowned as the Superintendant walked past them. Rachel was controlling the torch and shining it on the far wall. Closer to them James could see a pattern on the wall that reflected off the light and he wondered what it was.

But when he realised what they were, it was too late. The pattern was something he should have noticed before.

With an awful metallic shriek the Superintendant slammed an old rusty iron gate behind them, and with a wave of his hand they heard the ancient lock click – trapping them inside.

Rachel screamed so loudly that James had to cover his ears. But they were so far away from anyone else, and the small gap cleared between the rocks on the stairway barely allowed any sound to escape.

No one outside ever had a chance of hearing her.

CHAPTER FORTY-ONE

James ran to the bars and shook them violently. They rattled but the door wouldn't open.

"Let us out!" he yelled at the disappearing Superintendant, who was walking calmly back up the stairs. He spun around in shock and looked at Rachel. "You heard what he said," James said in total fear. "A flogging at first light! A ghost managed to hit me on the Isle and it really hurt," he groped at his shoulder and could feel a hefty bruise coming up. "If he's anything like the Nanny – which I think he is since he slammed that heavy door shut by himself, we're in *huge* trouble."

"Remember what the tour guide said at the very start when we were in the church?" Rachel said apprehensively. "Ghosts are strong enough to knock you out."

"Or, he won't come back at all," James sulked, "and we'll stay locked down here forever and die. So either way we need to find a way to get out right now."

Rachel shone her torch around the cell. Around three metres wide and four metres long, there was a stone bench at the back, with an old rag on it. The stone floor was damp, and water was beginning to run down into the cell.

"And if we don't get out of here soon we'll drown," Rachel joked poorly.

They paced around, trying to think of something. James examined the lock on the door, and saw that it was an old type that might be easy to pick. But there wasn't anything around the cell that he could use for a pick.

He looked down at the ground and saw what they had to work with: a piece of old cloth, a couple of leaves, some rocks, and a long, flat piece of metal.

As a nervous tick James picked the rocks up and began

banging them together. Suddenly a small spark was created and James dropped them to the ground in surprise.

"Brilliant! We can start a fire," he beamed a huge smile. "These rocks must be flint."

"Super. But what good will that do us?" Rachel asked. "Send smoke signals for help?"

But James didn't reply. Looking at the strip of metal, an idea was quickly forming in his mind.

"Chastity," he addressed the small ghost. "Can you move things?"

"Of course I can! I'm a big girl."

"Yes you are, sweetie," Rachel smiled. "*Ohhh*. Why don't we see if she can unlock the door? If the Superintendent can do it without a key, maybe she could too."

They ushered her towards the door and asked her to unlock it, but she couldn't. She simply didn't know how a lock worked, and their feeble attempts to explain didn't help either.

"Okay, that doesn't matter," James dismissed. "But can you pick up the rocks in my hand?" He held up the flint.

Chastity reached out and tried to pick the flint up, but her hands passed through the rock. She frowned. Still unaware that she was a ghost, she was unable to understand why she couldn't pick up a physical object.

"Concentrate really hard on feeling the rock and holding it," he instructed.

She did as she was told and the flint began wobbling in James' hand, and amazingly a few seconds later she picked it up.

"Well done!" Rachel praised her. "Now what?"

"Chastity, can you walk through the bars of the door?" James asked.

She glided through the door like it wasn't even there.

"Excellent. Now can you please go outside and pick up the biggest thing you see that will fit through the bars? Like a branch? Then bring it back here."

"Of course," Chastity exclaimed.

"Thank you so much," James smiled. With that she pranced

159

up the stairs, straight through the rocks, and vanished.

"Great. Now that you've lost the kid – who we need to save Tom and Edward, what are we going to do?" Rachel asked sarcastically.

James pointed at the lock on the door: "We're going to break that down."

She narrowed her eyes. "I think it'll take more than a branch. It may be old, but it's still fairly solid."

"Indeed it is," he said, putting on an English accent. "But, my dear Watson, look closer."

Rachel leaned forward and saw that the lock looked slightly blackened like it had been burnt. But she still didn't understand what he was on about.

"This is flint," James said, holding up the rocks. "And this metal is magnesium," he held up the paper-thin metal strip off the ground. "We're going to start a fire in the lock, put the magnesium in, and it'll soften up the metal. Magnesium burns at extremely high temperatures, and then we'll whack the lock with something hard – like a thick branch if Chastity brings one, or at worst we'll try kicking it. From the looks of the lock, some boy who was locked down here tried exactly the same thing. But he either wasn't strong enough to kick it down and escape himself, or he didn't have something to knock the lock with."

"I'm impressed, Sherlock," Rachel said, folding her arms. "Very impressed. How did you know all that stuff?"

"Dad is a geologist," he replied. "So through him I know a bit about rocks, minerals and metals."

She smiled. "So now we just wait for Chastity?"

"We start right away," he said, looking down at his watch. "It'll take a little while to heat the metal up."

He began by twisting off a small corner of the magnesium strip and dropping it into the keyhole. Then he stuffed a leaf into the lock as well to act as fuel and to get the temperature of the fire up. Next he bent off a few more corners of magnesium and gave them to Rachel to hold.

Finally he struck the pieces of flint together against a bit of the leaf that hung out of the keyhole. On the second strike the spark caught the leaf and a small fire started.

The fire slowly burned into the keyhole, and a couple of seconds later they heard a fizzling sound.

"It's working," James cried out. "The magnesium caught fire. Quickly, put another piece in there. No, put them all in!"

Careful not to burn her fingers, Rachel fed more pieces of magnesium into the keyhole, resulting in an even louder fizzle.

"Ouch," James exclaimed as he put a finger to the metal. "That's getting really hot."

They repeated the process over and over again – making the keyhole act like a mini furnace.

Chastity suddenly returned, dragging a straight branch through the hole in the rocks. It was about a metre long and about five centimetres in diameter. It weighed a couple of kilograms, so it was good and hardy.

"You're a lifesaver Chastity," Rachel beamed.

"I did well?" the young girl brightened.

"You did perfectly," James said as he continued working.

After a couple of minutes the metal around the keyhole was glowing dark orange. After adding another bit of magnesium, James grabbed the heavy branch and swung it as hard as he could straight at the lock. The loud clang bounced off the walls. He stopped and looked at the damage.

"It bent it! It really bent it."

He gave what remained of the magnesium strip to Rachel and told her to keep adding pieces, worried that the temperature could drop.

After every small piece Rachel put in, James swung the branch. It was almost as hard work as the rowing had been. The jarring from the branch hitting the metal lock hurt his entire body. At least he was sweating like a pig – the cold of outside completely forgotten.

As they were coming to the end of the magnesium, James swung again, and they heard a distinct metallic *crunck!* as the lock gave way. James immediately hit it again, and again, and then the lock fell to the floor, swinging the door open.

"*Yes*," they cried out aloud and hugged each other.

"Let's get out of here," James ordered, not wasting a moment.

CHAPTER FORTY-TWO

They scampered up the rocks in the stairway, and out into the open. It was still raining, but it had gone back down to a drizzle again, and more importantly the wind had died down. The storm had passed.

"Turn the torch off," James whispered to Rachel. "We don't want that crazy Superintendant to see us."

Maybe she turned it off too late, or maybe the Superintendant saw the pendant on Chastity's necklace glowing, but a cry went up from somewhere in the bush.

"Right, that'll be the end of you!" the Superintendant yelled out through the darkness. "Guards! Guards! After them!"

"Run," Rachel shrieked. Knowing that their escape had been spotted and that they couldn't just sneak off, she turned her flashlight back on. Not for the first time that night they raced through the bush and to the boat, leaping over rocks and fallen branches.

They hit the beach at full speed and once again James shoved the boat back into the water with Rachel at the oars.

Looking behind, they saw the Superintendant standing on the beach and throwing his hat to the sand and shaking his fist at them. Then he suddenly turned around and ran back towards Point Puer.

"He's up to something," James said with worry.

"Don't know, don't care," Rachel replied. "I'm going to take us to the nearest shore directly opposite us. If I'm right, that should land us behind the Commandant's House. It's too much of a risk to go back to the dockyards or the ferry terminal. By landing out of sight, the police won't see us. We've come too far to fail now."

"Then after we land we'll just leg it to the Penitentiary and reunite Chastity with her dad," James added.

"And then I'll be reunited with my nice warm bed," Rachel said dreamily between rows.

The bay was only choppy now, and the thunder was in the distance. By the time they hit land behind the Port Arthur settlement the rain had stopped entirely as well. James then decided to end his humiliating experience in the pink jacket, and changed back into his shirt and jacket. They were still damp, but he hoped that his body warmth would dry them out.

They tied the boat to a tree and cautiously made their way through a thicket of trees towards the Commandant's House.

Breaking through the trees at the back of the house, thankfully they weren't challenged by the Commandant or even more worryingly, the Nanny.

In the distance they both swore they could hear gunfire and wondered what that was about. But it was none of their concern and they continued, quietly gaining confidence with every step as they got closer and closer to the Penitentiary.

Walking up to the Guard House, Rachel began quietly talking. "You know, we've barely had a chance to actually talk at all tonight. After all of this is over and you go back to Brisbane, we should talk over the 'Net or something."

"I'd like that," he replied with a smile. But just as he said that, somewhere below them they heard the static crackle of a radio.

"Boss, it's me, Percy," they heard the radio blare. "I can't see them anywhere."

"Shut up you idiot," the policeman below them at the bottom of the steps – in front of the condemned cell – replied. "I think I just heard something."

"That would just be the static at the start of the transmission – radios do that," the other policeman replied.

"No you fool – before then. Just shut up, I'll get back to you. I'm going to investigate."

James quickly waved his hands to get them to retreat back. They couldn't go to the Commandant's House for obvious reasons, so their only option was to run away from their objective

– the Penitentiary – and instead go across the field towards the Hospital.

"This is not good," Rachel panted as they ran – still exhausted after her rowing.

When they reached the Hospital they were surprised by the lack of ghosts. Surely a lot of people would have died there, so there would be a lot of ghosts attached to the building, but only a handful wandered around – seemingly not even noticing the boy and two girls running through the old ruin.

James looked behind and saw that the policeman had turned his torch on and was running across the field as well.

A glance to their left showed that the other, larger policeman had also turned his flashlight on and was coming towards them from the direction of the Penitentiary. *They'd set a trap and waited for us in the dark*, James realised.

"Oh God, do you think they've seen us?" Rachel asked in horror. Just as before, Chastity looked thrilled by the chase; it was all a game to her.

"I don't know," James frantically replied. "I think they're just chasing after our sounds."

Looking around, they only had one option for escape: running across the bridge over the river and towards the Asylum. Otherwise they'd be trapped in the middle between the police.

"Quickly, over there," James pointed at the bridge. Barely taking notice, they ran past the ruins of the Paupers' Mess where Tom had seen out the final years of his life as an old man after he'd been given his freedom.

"Oh no," James moaned as they ran up to the Asylum. "I'm not going in there again with that crazy ghost after we've seen what they're capable of."

"Then our only option is the Separate Prison," Rachel said with surprising calmness. But that quickly changed when she turned around. "Hurry up. I can see their torches again."

But James stayed rooted to the spot for a second longer. He saw the second policeman running across another bridge. It meant that the police could work together to trap them from two sides.

"We're done for..." he whispered before running after Rachel and Chastity into the Separate Prison.

CHAPTER FORTY-THREE

When they ran inside the building it was deathly silent. James had briefly read about the Separate Prison from his information brochure when they'd first visited the Asylum. He remembered that the two buildings were horribly linked.

The Separate Prison was usually where convicts risked going mad to begin with. As punishment they were put under horrible restrictions where they weren't allowed to talk to anyone else. Their names were never used for as long as they were inside the building. They were only called by a number. When they went outside of their cells they had to wear a hood that covered their face. Their identity was completely removed.

What remained of the Separate Prison was two main wings – A and C Wing, with cells on both sides of the wide stone corridors. The cells in C Wing were unrestored and bare – though the roof was still in place all over the building, and visitors could walk straight into the individual cells. A Wing was completely restored, with full period furniture and doors.

The kids ran into the abandoned C Wing section of the building. Ghosts stared at them from almost every cell.

"I'm not getting into a cell with them," Rachel said in disgust to cancel that idea before James could suggest it.

They jogged down the corridor and into a middle chamber with a raised ceiling. From there they saw that there were three exits: one that they came from – which would be covered by the policeman who chased them over the field, and two more on the other side, which the second officer would see them use if they left that way.

"We're trapped," James said in alarm. He looked down at Chastity and saw that even she was beginning to look scared – finally realising that she might not get to see her father after all.

Rachel looked behind them and saw a set of stairs to another doorway. "The chapel! Of course; I forgot all about it. I never got to see it," she explained. "It was being renovated when I was here the last time."

"Is there another exit through the chapel?"

"I don't know. Hopefully," she said.

They ran up a small set of stairs to the chapel and flashed their remaining torch.

James' heart sank. "It's a dead end!"

But within the chapel, salvation was at hand.

It was Captain Hunter and the two Privates – the cheerful soldiers they'd met earlier after being challenged by them on their way to see Daegan the blacksmith.

Before the kids could say anything they heard a large *bang* and a *clang* as heavy doors on either end of the prison building were opened and then closed.

"James Masters and Rachel Peters!" It was the voice of the older policeman who'd been just metres away from them at the Guard Tower. "We know you're in here. We've spent a lot of time looking for you, and frankly I think you've been trying to elude us. But the game is up. You're trapped. Show yourselves!"

From their position inside the chapel, neither of them was within the police officers' vision. But they could see the light of their two torches from separate ends of A and C wings.

"Have it your way. We will find you," the older policemen said aloud. "Percy! You know what to do – check all of the cells."

"Okay boss," the podgy second officer called back.

They heard the policemen's heavy steps echoing through the building.

With no time to lose, Rachel and James spun around to talk to Captain Hunter.

"You've got to help us," James urgently whispered to the soldiers. "We're being chased, and those two men are trying to keep Chastity away from her dad, Edward Burke. Tom sent us to help them."

"Is that true little lady?" Captain Hunter asked gently to

Chastity, getting down onto his knee in front of her.

"Yes sir," she replied in her tiny voice.

"Well then," he jumped up. "We were just on our way to fix up a ruckus outside, but it's our sworn duty to serve and protect Her Majesty's subjects." He looked at James and Rachel. "We'll see what we can do."

The two policemen's footsteps were painfully close now. The police could have only been ten metres away, and right at the end of the wings – directly before the centre chamber where the entrance to the chapel was.

The three soldiers ran out of the chapel and the kids heard Captain Hunter shouting out to the convicts in their cells.

"Look here you mongrels," Captain Hunter called to the convicts in the cells. "What's it like to spend eternity in this Godforsaken hellhole of a building with weasels for company?"

Throughout the building convict ghosts stood up and took notice.

One of the convicts in the restored A Wing began banging loudly on his cell door.

"*What is that?*" one of the policemen – Constable Percy – yelled in surprise.

"Relax," Sergeant Cooper soothed from the other side of the chamber. "They're just trying to play with our minds. We've got them now."

Percy's voice wavered. "But that's coming from an empty cell that I just checked..."

Another one of the soldier's took his superior's actions to heart, cruelly yelling out: "Every day we punished you in life was a day I cherished!"

More banging on doors and walls from the convicts.

The policemen spun around, actually able to hear a convict howling.

Bang! Bang! Bang! Crunch! One of the convicts in A Wing broke down his door and tore into the corridor, wanting to tear the soldiers apart. Constable Percy just happened to be in his way.

Percy heard the running footsteps behind him. He swung his

torch around but only saw an empty corridor. There was no one there.

Or was there?

The sound of running kept on coming – closer and closer.

Whimpering, he held his ground bravely for a full second before his courage shattered and he broke into a full sprint – racing towards the nearest exit and screaming at the top of his lungs.

Sergeant Cooper looked on in terror as his fellow officer and son-in-law bolted out of the building. He'd also heard the sound of running, but wasn't sure where it came from.

"If it looks like a convict, and smells like a convict: it must be a convict!" the last soldier yelled.

The taunting caused another convict to run screaming out of his cell – this time from C Wing. Right behind Sergeant Cooper.

Once again the sound of the convict's shoes pounding down the corridor echoed through the building.

Cooper spun around and shone his torch down the corridor – expecting to see someone running towards him.

But there was only empty air.

Yet another convict burst out of his cell – right next to Cooper, and he felt wind moving as the invisible convict rushed past.

Like Percy, his resolve only lasted a second as the running came closer and closer and was right on him. He scrambled out of the prison with flailing arms and legs. "*Aaarrrggghhhhhh!*" the sounds of his screaming disappeared far into the night...

With both policemen gone, the convict ghosts charged at the soldiers at full pace and dived, only to fly straight through them.

"You dumb brutes," Captain Hunter scolded. "You're as dead as we are – you can't do anything to us."

The convicts picked themselves up and snarled at them, circling around.

"Ahh!" one of them said. "But we can do something to the pretty little ones." He pointed towards James and Rachel.

Captain Hunter swallowed nervously, but gathered his

composure. "But there is a difference between you convict spirits and us: we can leave this building. You are trapped forever."

They hissed and spat at his face.

Captain Hunter swiftly turned around and waved James, Rachel and Chastity towards the door. "Come quickly children," he whispered to them. "You're in great danger here."

CHAPTER FORTY-FOUR

They all ran out of the Separate Prison and into the intersection of Champ and Tarleton Street where they were met by an extraordinary sight.

In the field next to the Government Gardens, a battle was raging between convicts and soldiers.

"I told you that there was ruckus about," Captain Hunter laughed. "Have a look at them!"

Just like at the Separate Prison, the convicts were charging at their former guards. There were about a hundred ghosts and twenty soldiers. They took swings at each other that didn't hit anything, and fired guns with bullets that struck nothing as well. It was a complete stalemate – they simply couldn't do anything to each other.

The Captain chuckled again. "I wonder what caused it? It's never happened before – not on this scale anyway."

James and Rachel shuffled uncomfortably. "I think we're responsible," James said, and then quickly explained what had happened on the Isle of the Dead. "It must have spread to over here. Some of the ghosts must be able to travel between the Isle and here."

Captain Hunter nodded. "Aye, some can. And I should have half a mind to arrest you two for causing a public disturbance." He laughed and grinned at the two Privates beside him.

"Thank you so much for helping us with those two men," Rachel said. "But now we need to get Chastity to the Penitentiary."

"We will escort you," the Captain replied.

"But don't you need to sort out the ... err ... ruckus?" James asked.

The Captain turned around. "Who? Them? They'll get bored soon enough once they finally realise they can't actually hit each other. The fools! Besides, there might be trouble in the Penitentiary as well, so it would be best if we came with you."

James and Rachel hadn't thought of that. If the ghost war had spread to the mainland then they could be in trouble anywhere at Port Arthur. They eagerly nodded, happy for the assistance.

They quickly walked the short distance to the main prison building, and James looked over his shoulder in worry. The night sky was turning ever lighter shades of blue. Dawn was almost upon them.

Entering the Penitentiary, they saw that it was emptier than before. Some of the ghosts inside must have left to join the battle outside.

"You're back!" bellowed the convict who had scared Rachel earlier.

"And you never left!" she wise-cracked in return, resulting in a snarl from the ghost. "Toodles!" she waved him goodbye without looking back.

They went up the stairs quickly to the place where they had seen Edward Burke. Rachel could sense Chastity holding her hand tightly.

But Edward was gone.

"No. No, it can't be," James moaned. "It's not fair! It isn't dawn yet..."

They looked around, but Chastity's father was nowhere to be seen.

Suddenly Tom appeared in the middle of the group.

"Uncle Thomas!" Chastity yelled, running up and hugging him – a family bond uniting them in a way so they could hold each other while the other ghosts couldn't even touch each other.

"Sweetheart! You have no idea how much I missed you," Tom cooed, bringing a tear to Rachel's eye. "You have grown so much since I last saw you."

But he let go of her quickly and turned to the others with a serious look on his face. "There is no time left. Edward has gone to the church to pray before he leaves on his journey."

James looked straight up into the sky, through the gaping

hole where the roof once stood. Light was creeping further and further, and it was becoming brighter by the second.

Without a word, all seven of them ran down the stairs and left the Penitentiary.

They ran as fast as they could with Chastity past the waterfront – careful to keep a wide berth from the continuing fighting in the field.

But just as they reached Tarleton Street at the base of the Government Gardens – with the lit-up church well in sight, they were forced to a halt.

"You, soldiers! Arrest those children!"

The Superintendant of Point Puer stood between them and their objective, holding an old pistol and pointing it straight at them.

CHAPTER FORTY-FIVE

"I've got you now," the Superintendant said proudly. "Soldiers, arrest these criminals and lock them up."

James looked behind and saw the first sign of the sun flickering through the trees behind the church.

Captain Hunter stood up straight and saluted. "Don't you worry, sir, we're just taking them with us now. We were on our way to the Magistrate's to see to their paperwork."

"What!" Rachel exclaimed in surprise. But Private Marks slyly winked at her.

"There's no need to worry yourself Superintendant. We caught them trying to pass stolen goods to the other prisoners in the Penitentiary – including him," Hunter pointed at Tom – who then hung his head, trying to look guilty.

"I want to see them hang!" the Superintendant fumed.

"Can't guarantee that, sir, but I'm sure they'll get a few more years added to their sentence, and a good lashing. Why are you so concerned about them anyway, sir?"

"They esca– they *stole* from my personal quarters," the ghost quickly covered-up to hide the embarrassment of their crafty getaway from the underground cell.

"A most heinous crime if there ever were one, sir," Captain Hunter shook his head. "But it's far too early in the day to be worrying yourself with them. They'll get what's coming to them, I assure you."

"I look forward to it!" The Superintendant spat at their feet, and stomped off towards the docks without a farewell.

"I've always hated that man," Private Marks sighed.

"Me too," Private Spencer said sourly.

"And I," Captain Hunter nodded his head. "Never have I met a less considerate person in my life – and afterlife."

"Then again, you've never met my mother in law!" Private Spencer quipped.

"Wait until you hear about mine!" Captain Hunter retorted with laughter and faced the others. "You four go to the church and finish your business. We've got work to do I'm afraid. But you'll be fine now."

"Thank you so much," Rachel said.

"Think nothing of it, miss," he bowed graciously. "Thank you and good day. I hope we can meet again someday," the soldier replied.

Captain Hunter turned around and the two Privates tipped their hats and followed him towards the field of fighting. They heard the soldiers begin to exchange family stories, and the sound of their laughter carried on into the early hours.

CHAPTER FORTY-SIX

They ran into the church just in time.

Edward was at the front, carrying a dirty sack over his shoulder and just picking himself up from his knees to leave on his one year journey to England and back.

"Daddy!" Chastity screamed the moment she saw him, sprinting across the church.

He spun around in surprise at her voice, and his face registered pure shock. She vaulted up at him, and as they embraced a blinding white light exploded from them, causing James and Rachel to cover their eyes. A split second later the light disappeared and Edward had transformed.

He was now clean; shaven and his hair cut back. Gone was the soot and coal from his face, and he wore a pristine white shirt and brown trousers – exactly like his brother. Tom walked up to him and they embraced; tears flowing down their cheeks. The family resemblance was now clear.

"Thank you, thank you so much brother," Edward said. "How did you find Chastity?"

"It wasn't me," Tom replied. He pointed towards James and Rachel. "They did it."

Edward came over to them and moved to shake their hands, before realising it was not actually possible.

"H-How? W-Why did you do this?"

Rachel answered with a smile. "Your brother found us. When we found out your story we would've done anything to help you, Chastity and Tom."

"You children are incredible," Edward said, still in disbelief. "I would have been trapped forever in my madness trying to find her."

"Don't worry," James assured. "You have Chastity now, and

where you're going, your wife will be waiting too."

"If she can ever forgive me for abandoning her and Chastity," he began sobbing.

Tom stepped forward and put his hands on his brother's shoulders. "You never abandoned her. It was my fault. It was all my fault that you went to Port Arthur. We are a family cursed... At least, we were until James and Rachel came along. Now we are one," he smiled towards them.

Chastity ran up and hugged Rachel; she could feel warmth run through her body and couldn't help but to cry.

"Thank you for giving me my Daddy back," Chastity whispered, her eyes glistening as the streaks of light broke into the sky above. "I want you to have my necklace," she smiled, taking it off and putting it in Rachel's hand.

Her mouth quivering, Rachel was lost for words and couldn't speak, and James only managed a weak "You're welcome" on her behalf before he began choking-up as well.

Tom ushered his family to stand side by side. "Your wife will understand and all will be well, especially when you bring her a little treasure," he said to his brother, stroking Chastity's hair to reassure her as well. "Go now, and I will join you there in a moment."

Chastity and Edward smiled at James and Rachel one last time before shimmering into a pair of lights and shooting around the spires of the church and disappearing into the sky.

"And now, for you two," Tom said, his voice and English accent trembling. "You gave me a gift I can never repay. You saved my brother, found my darling niece, and by uniting them you freed me from the bonds of my oath to remain here until they were saved. Not only do I owe you for reuniting my family; I owe you my own soul."

Rachel and James could only blush.

"I have nothing to give you but a promise," Tom said. "If you ever require my help, I will be there to assist you."

With that, he smiled and was gone in a dazzling light; all the colours of the rainbow dancing like water reflecting on a wall.

"Wow. Just ... wow," James said, his legs suddenly feeling like jelly. He sat down on the grass inside the church. Rachel sat down beside him and stared off into the distance.

Neither spoke until they heard a shout right outside the church walls. "I swear I saw a light there!" a man exclaimed. They both recognised the voice.

They heard a number of feet shuffling on the gravel outside.

"We're in for it now," James said, too exhausted to attempt another escape.

"Mmm..." Rachel yawned, accepting their fates.

The two policemen ran into the church, followed by both sets of their parents.

"There they are," Constable Percy exclaimed in delight.

"You!" Sergeant Cooper cried out. "We've been chasing you all night."

"Oh, really?" Rachel said innocently, crossing her arms. "Like where?"

"You know exactly where! For starters we almost had you in the Separate Prison just before."

"How come you didn't catch us then?" she said bravely.

"Gho–" Constable Percy began before being cut-off by his superior officer and father-in-law.

"–*That* isn't important. What *is* important though is that we finally caught you."

"Oh leave them alone, you big bully!" James' mother scolded the officer and ran up to her son, smothering him with hugs and kisses. For now she didn't seem to care that he was cold and damp.

"*Mum!*" He could see Rachel giggling at him while he tried wriggling out of her bear-like grip. "Oh jeez."

But then Rachel's parents ran up to her as well, and it was James' turn to laugh at her expense.

"Where on earth were you?" his dad asked with his baby sister cradled in his arms. "We were worried sick about you."

"Well, there's a perfectly rational explanation," James said.

Rachel stared at him in astonishment with an *oh-this-is-going-to-*

be-good look on her face.

"We discovered a blacksmith's tool set, and a previously unknown part of the ruins," he said matter-of-factly.

"Excuse me?" an unknown voice from behind asked. A woman wearing an official Port Arthur site shirt walked up to the group. "What did you kids say?"

"We found a set of old blacksmith's tools buried in the Government Gardens, and a previously undiscovered underground chamber out at Point Puer boys' prison," Rachel replied in turn.

The woman's jaw dropped in barely contained excitement. "*This* I've got to see!"

James grinned back at her. "Seeing *is* believing."